THE BOBBSEY TWINS
AND THE BIG RIVER MYSTERY

A two-weeks' visit with Aunt Alice on her private island in the Hudson River is an exciting prospect for the Bobbsey twins. The more exciting because Bert, Nan, Freddie, and Flossie know that Aunt Alice plans to give each of them a special present—just because she loves them.

But the twins naturally seem to attract adventure. Imagine their surprise when they learn that the U. S. Customs Service has its eye on the island, looking for smugglers. Puzzling, too, is the disappearance of a big wooden crate containing their great-great-aunt's valuable heirlooms.

The twins don't spend all their time investigating clues. There's too much to do—with a whole island, a boat, a historic river, and a new "treasure" at every turn.

A night's camp-out unravels one puzzling mystery, but it takes a trip all the way down the Hudson to New York City to solve the other. And the third mystery—why Aunt Alice doesn't give them their presents—they're too polite to ask, of course—has a happy ending too!

THE BOBBSEY TWINS BOOKS
By Laura Lee Hope

"Look! A box with straps on it!"

The Bobbsey Twins and the Big River Mystery

By

LAURA LEE HOPE

GROSSET & DUNLAP

Publishers   *New York*

PRINTED IN THE UNITED STATES OF AMERICA

The Bobbsey Twins and the Big River Mystery

CONTENTS

CHAPTER I

A ROCKY BOAT RIDE

"WE'RE going for a visit on a bee-yoo-ti-ful island!" sang out blond, blue-eyed Flossie Bobbsey gaily.

She was gazing at the Hudson River from the rear seat of the family station wagon.

"And get the presents Aunt Alice has for us," said her six-year-old twin, Freddie. He was alongside Flossie. The little boy grinned. "I wonder what the presents are!"

"I hope mine's a new doll," Flossie remarked.

Her sister, Nan, who was in the middle seat, turned around. She was twelve, and had dark hair and eyes. "Even if it is a doll, Flossie, it won't be new. Aunt Alice wrote Mother that she was moving away from her island and giving us some of the things she's had for years and years!"

"Oh!" Flossie said. "Well, old dolls can be fun to play with, too!"

Next to Nan was Bert, Nan's twin, who looked like her. "I hope we can go fishing while we're there. I brought our gear."

Mr. Bobbsey, at the wheel, chuckled. "You find out where the fish are, Bert," he said jokingly. "When I come back to pick up my family, you can show me where to catch the biggest ones!"

Bert agreed laughingly, then spoke to his pretty mother, seated beside Mr. Bobbsey. "Why doesn't Aunt Alice want to live on her island any longer?" he asked.

"She has been in the big house a long time," Mrs. Bobbsey reminded him. "Now that she's getting old, Aunt Alice thinks she'd like to have an apartment in New York City."

Mrs. Bobbsey and the children planned to spend two weeks of their summer vacation with Mrs. Bobbsey's great-aunt, Miss Alice Conover, whose old house was on an island in the great river.

"Does Aunt Alice live on the island all alone, Mommy?" Flossie asked, looking worried.

"No, dear," her mother said. "Toony and Trudy are with her."

Flossie giggled. "Who are Toony and Trudy?"

Mrs. Bobbsey said they were Tunis Staats and his wife, Gertrude. Toony took care of the island grounds and ran Aunt Alice's boat, while Trudy did the cooking and housework.

"They belong to one of the old Dutch families that settled along the Hudson River back in the seventeenth century," Mrs. Bobbsey said. "Henry Hudson, who first explored the river, claimed the land for Holland, and many Dutch people came over to make their homes here."

Freddie looked puzzled. "Toony and Trudy must be awf'ly old if they came from Holland that long ago," he said.

Mr. Bobbsey laughed. "Your mother didn't mean Toony and Trudy came from Holland, my little fat fireman," he said. "It was their great-great-great-great-grandparents!"

"Oh!" said Freddie in relief. His father liked to call him "little fat fireman," because Freddie was very fond of playing with his toy fire engine and planned to become a fireman when he grew up.

The twins again discussed the presents which Aunt Alice had promised them. Freddie was sure one of them would be an old-time fire wagon!

A short time later Mr. Bobbsey slowed the car. "Anybody hungry?" he called.

"I'm starved!" Freddie replied.

"So am I!" Flossie agreed with a giggle.

"How about it, Mary?" Mr. Bobbsey asked his wife. "Shall we stop at this restaurant for lunch?" He indicated a low white building ahead.

The twins' mother nodded. "I think it would be a good idea, Dick. We have plenty of time. Toony is to pick us up at the River Edge dock at three, and we're only a couple of hours from there now."

Mr. Bobbsey pulled into the crowded parking area and found a space. The family piled out and hurried toward the restaurant. When they walked into the cool dining room there were only two empty booths. The small twins quickly slid into one of them.

"Bert and I will take the other booth, Mother, if you and Dad want to sit with Freddie and Flossie," Nan offered.

"All right, dear," her mother agreed.

"I'll have strawberry ice cream!" Flossie announced a moment later as she took a paper napkin from the container.

Mrs. Bobbsey laughed. "I think you'd better have something before ice cream," she said. "How about a chicken sandwich?"

Flossie agreed, and her father ordered lunch for them all. Bert and Nan chattered busily as they munched their sandwiches. Suddenly Bert motioned to his twin.

"Listen!" he whispered.

Two men were seated in the booth behind Nan. Bert could see their heads. One was gray-haired, the other was blond. Their voices, while not loud, could be heard easily by the two children.

"I'm sure there's smuggling going on along the river," one man was saying, "but we haven't been able to learn how it's being done or who's doing it."

"Haven't you any idea?" his companion asked.

"No," the first voice replied. "That's why I'm up here—to find out."

Nan's brown eyes were wide with excitement. Bert started to say something, but at that moment Mr. Bobbsey stopped at their booth.

"If you've finished lunch, we'll go," he said.

Reluctantly the older twins followed the others from the restaurant. They all piled into the station wagon. As Bert started to close the door, the two men came from the building. The gray-haired one was of medium height. His friend was taller and younger.

The older man held a sheet of white paper in his hand and was talking intently. Bert and Nan watched the men with interest. They turned toward a black sedan parked nearby.

At that moment a puff of wind caught the

white paper and tore it from the man's grasp. It fluttered in the breeze and came straight toward the station wagon.

"I'll get it!" Bert called, jumping from the car. With a flying leap he grabbed the paper as it was about to blow onto the highway.

The two men ran up. "Thank you, son!" the gray-haired one exclaimed, taking the paper from Bert. "That's an important memorandum, and I wouldn't want to lose it."

By this time Nan had joined her twin. "My brother and I couldn't help overhearing your talk in the restaurant about smuggling. It sounded very exciting. And—well—we like mysteries."

The men smiled at her. "My name is John Ward," the older one said. "I'm with the United States Customs Service. This is Mr. Smith, a local detective. The Customs Service tries to catch people who are cheating the government. It can be very exciting at times. This paper your brother rescued for me contains a list of articles which are being brought into our country without payment of duty."

"I'm glad it didn't blow away," Bert remarked. He introduced himself and his sister.

"Are you on your way to New York City?" Mr. Ward asked.

"I'll get it!" Bert called

When Bert explained that the Bobbsey children were going to visit their great-aunt on an island in the river, the Customs man looked thoughtful. "Will you do a favor for me?" he asked.

"Sure!" Bert replied eagerly. "What is it?"

Mr. Ward took a card from his pocket and wrote on it. Then he handed it to Bert. "If you see anything suspicious along the Hudson, will you call me at this telephone number?"

Bert and Nan, feeling very proud of doing such a job, quickly promised. They said good-by to the men and hurried back to the station wagon.

"Guess what!" cried Bert, as his father started off. "Nan and I are detectives now!" He told the others what Mr. Ward had said about smuggling on the river.

"Flossie and I'll help you look for the bad men!" Freddie assured Bert. As his twin nodded vigorously, the others laughed.

"Good for you!" said Mr. Bobbsey.

They made excellent time and shortly before three o'clock pulled up to the River Edge dock. As they stopped, a short, blond man arose from a piling on which he had been seated and walked over to the station wagon.

"You must be the Bobbseys," he said with a broad smile. "I'm Toony Staats, and Miss

Conover's boat is over there." He pointed to a trim white motor launch beside the dock.

"Wow!" Bert exclaimed admiringly. "What a neat boat!"

"The *White Gull*'s a good craft!" Toony agreed proudly. "But I guess she'll be sold when Miss Conover moves to New York City," he added sadly.

Mr. Bobbsey introduced his family, then helped Toony carry the luggage over to the boat.

"Sorry I can't stay, Mary," he said when everything had been stowed on the launch. "I hope my business won't take too long. I should be back here to pick you up in about two weeks." He shook hands with Toony, kissed his family, and got back into the car.

"Good-by, Daddy!" the children chorused as he drove away. They waved until he was out of sight, then followed Toony to the boat.

A steady wind blew in off the river as the *White Gull* pulled away from the dock. White-capped waves slapped against the hull, and the boat rocked from side to side.

"Goodness!" Mrs. Bobbsey exclaimed. "I didn't know the river ever became this rough. Is—is it safe?"

Toony smiled. "Oh my, yes. You might say that the Hudson's really a branch of the ocean.

We get tides all the way up to Albany. The tide's coming in now, and with this wind added, we'll have a bouncy ride. But we'll make it!"

Flossie was very solemn. Her yellow curls blew in the stiff breeze and her cheeks turned pink with concern. Nan looked worried too, as she pulled a scarf from a coat pocket and tied it over her head.

"Yonder's Conover Island!" Toony cried.

The Bobbseys saw a small wooded island. The northern side had a tiny stretch of sandy beach while the southern end was steep and rocky. A white house could be seen dimly through the trees directly ahead.

In another few minutes Toony brought the *White Gull* up to a small dock. He threw a rope over a piling and jumped out. "Not very far to step when the tide's in!" he said cheerily, stretching out a hand toward Mrs. Bobbsey to help her alight.

The children then scrambled out onto the dock. Toony lifted out the suitcases to Bert. Suddenly a surprised look came over the man's round face.

"What's the matter?" Flossie asked him.

"Why, a box of valuables I left here on the dock is gone!" he exclaimed worriedly. "Gone! Someone must have stolen it!"

"The smugglers!" cried Freddie.

CHAPTER II

THE MYSTERY VISITOR

"WHAT box?" Bert asked.

"Miss Conover's box from the museum," Toony replied. "The mail boat left it just as I was starting out to meet you. I planned to carry it up to the house when I got back. Freddie, what's this about smugglers?"

Bert explained, and Toony frowned. "I suppose a person who would try to cheat Uncle Sam out of money could be a thief too."

Mrs. Bobbsey said kindly, "Perhaps Miss Conover sent someone to pick up the package."

"Well, we'll see," Toony answered hopefully. He motioned the Bobbseys to follow him up a winding path.

The walk was edged with big stones painted white. On the green lawn in front of the house stood a large iron dog. He seemed to be looking out over the river.

11

When Flossie saw the statue, she ran over and threw her arms around it. "He looks just like Snap!" she cried. "Only he can't wag his tail."

Back in Lakeport where the Bobbseys lived, the children had three pets. The oldest was Snap, a shaggy white dog who had once belonged to a circus. Then there was the frisky fox terrier, Waggo, and Snoop, the black cat. The twins had been sorry to leave their pets behind, but Dinah and Sam Johnson, the jolly colored couple who helped Mr. and Mrs. Bobbsey, had promised to take good care of them.

Now Nan stopped short in the middle of the path as she looked at the Conover house. "It has eight sides!" she exclaimed in amazement.

The white house had a wide porch which ran all the way around. On the roof was an eight-sided cupola.

The front door opened, and two women hurried out. One was tall and dignified-looking. She had snowy-white hair. The other was small and wiry and had snapping black eyes.

"You're surprised at my house?" the older woman asked with a smile.

"It's the first octagonal house the twins have ever seen, Aunt Alice," Mrs. Bobbsey said as she kissed her great-aunt.

One by one the children were introduced to

Miss Conover and then to the younger woman, who proved to be Trudy, Toony's wife.

"Eight-sided houses were very popular along the Hudson River over a hundred years ago," Aunt Alice explained.

Trudy spoke up with a twinkle in her eyes. "They don't have any dark corners in them, so the goblins have no place to hide!"

The twins laughed. They knew there were no goblins and that Trudy was teasing.

Toony cleared his throat nervously. "Did you bring that box up from the dock, Trudy?"

"No, I didn't," Trudy answered.

Aunt Alice looked worried. "Was it the box from the museum, Toony?" she asked.

Toony nodded. "I was going to bring it up when I got back from River Edge. I figured it'd be perfectly safe on the dock, but it's gone!" he said.

"What was in the box, Aunt Alice?" Mrs. Bobbsey asked sympathetically.

"Two of my most valuable possessions," the elderly woman replied. "A fashion doll and a wooden flute which belonged to our family in the time of the Revolutionary War."

"What's a fashion doll?" Flossie asked.

Aunt Alice explained that many years ago, before there were fashion magazines, dressmakers in Paris, France, used to send dolls around the world to show people the latest dress styles.

"My doll had a silk gown with a train and a little straw bonnet tied with a bow under her chin," Aunt Alice said.

"She must be bee-yoo-ti-ful!" Flossie sighed.

"I lent the doll and the flute to a museum in New York City. The director wrote that the things were being returned, carefully packed in a wooden box, and would reach me today."

Flossie looked at Freddie. She could tell he had the same thought. Were the doll and the flute the presents Aunt Alice had planned to give them? The small twins looked sad.

"Shouldn't you call the police, Aunt Alice?" Bert spoke up. "Maybe they can find the box."

The elderly woman looked relieved. "Thank you, Bert," she said. "Of course, that's what I should do. I'll call right away. Do come in. Trudy will show you to your rooms."

When Miss Conover had gone inside to the telephone, Toony looked at his wife. "I have an idea who took that box," he said.

"Who?"

"I passed Slippery Jenks on my way to River Edge. He had a big package in his boat. It could've been Miss Conover's box!"

"Is Slippery Jenks a smuggler?" Freddie asked eagerly.

"Not that I know of." Toony explained that before coming to work for Miss Conover, he had been a riverboat captain. Jenks had been a sailor on his boat. Toony had discharged him for stealing, and Slippery had been trying to make trouble for Toony ever since.

"Where does this Slippery Jenks live?" Bert asked.

"Let's go find him!" Freddie cried at the same time.

Toony told the twins that Slippery Jenks had a house in River Edge. "But it's too late to go back over there now," he added.

"We'll help you find the box," Flossie assured the man. "We're good at solving mysteries!"

Flossie was right. In *The Goldfish Mystery* the twins had gone to Japan with their parents, and during their visit had recovered a valuable bracelet which had been stolen from their hostess. And in *Volcano Land* they had found an ancient statue for a little Hawaiian girl.

By this time the Bobbseys had come inside the house. As Bert helped Toony carry in the luggage, he could see that a stairway ran up through the center of the house to the cupola at the top. There were five large rooms on each floor, circling the stairwell.

"I like a house with lots of sides!" Flossie

declared, following her mother and Trudy up the stairs.

The children were tired from all the excitement of the day and went to bed soon after supper that evening. Bert had been asleep for some time when suddenly a noise awakened him. He listened carefully. "It sounds like oars splashing!" he thought.

Slipping quietly out of bed, he went to the window and peered out into the darkness. As he looked, Bert saw a movement among the bushes by the water's edge. Who could it be?

"What's the matter, Bert?" came his brother's sleepy voice from the other bed.

Before replying, Bert put on his robe and slippers. "Go back to sleep, Freddie," he whispered. "I think I see someone out there in the bushes. I'm going to see who it is."

"Not without me!" Freddie said indignantly. He was wide awake by this time.

"All right," Bert replied. "Hurry up!"

A minute later the two boys were tiptoeing down the long flight of stairs to the first floor. They found a side door and crept out onto the porch.

The grounds appeared to be deserted. "I don't see anyone," Freddie whispered.

Bert put up a warning hand. "Wait!"

The boys stood still a minute, then Freddie

grabbed Bert. "Look!" he breathed. A flashlight shone for a second in the bushes, then went out.

"I'm going to investigate," Bert said in a low tone. "You'd better stay here."

"I'm going too!" Freddie declared stubbornly.

"Okay, but keep behind me."

The boys walked silently down the steps and out onto the lawn. They ran across the grass until they reached the shelter of the trees. Both could see the shadowy figure of a man moving along the edge of the sandy beach.

"Come on, let's get him!" Bert cried.

The boys dashed toward the beach. They leaped toward the man, and each grabbed one of his arms. But the next minute he shook himself free and ran across the narrow strip of sand. The stranger jumped into a boat and rowed rapidly away.

"I'll bet he was looking for something," Bert said, puzzled. "But what?"

"There's something spooky on the island!" Freddie cried excitedly. "Maybe he was hunting for a treasure!"

The brothers could find no clues to the strange man, so they went back to bed. The next morning they could hardly wait until everyone had gathered at the breakfast table.

"You look as if you're bursting to tell something, Freddie!" Mrs. Bobbsey remarked with a smile. "What is it?"

"Bert and I almost caught a burglar last night!" Freddie cried.

"A burglar!" Aunt Alice exclaimed. "How could there be a burglar on my island?"

"He came in a rowboat," Bert said. "But he was a queer sort of burglar. He was looking in the bushes instead of in the house!"

"You'd better tell us all about it, boys," Mrs. Bobbsey urged.

When the story was finished, Aunt Alice looked mystified. "I can't understand what the man could have been searching for."

"Let's go out and look for clues!" Nan proposed, jumping up from her chair.

"Finish your breakfast first," Mrs. Bobbsey said firmly.

When the last bites of toast had been taken, Bert stood up. "All right, Bobbsey detectives. On the job!"

The four children ran outdoors and down toward the little beach. They began to push aside branches and peer at the ground underneath. Nothing unusual came to light.

"I can't imagine what the man was after!" Bert finally declared in disgust. "There's certainly nothing here!"

Nan had wandered to the beach. There were signs of scuffed footprints in the sand. "Is this where you caught him?" she called.

"Yes." Bert walked toward her as Nan continued to look at the prints. Suddenly she stooped and picked up something she had seen.

"What's this?" She held out a round piece of metal to her twin.

"It's a silver button!" Bert exclaimed. "It must have fallen off the man's jacket when Freddie and I grabbed him last night!"

"Come on," Nan urged. "Let's see if Aunt Alice recognizes this!"

In a few minutes the twins dashed into the dining room where Aunt Alice and Mrs. Bobbsey were still seated. Breathlessly Nan handed the button to the elderly woman.

"Do you know whose this is?" she cried.

Aunt Alice took the button and turned it over in her hand. "No," she replied, "but what a lovely design is carved on it! It looks Indian."

At that moment Toony came in from the kitchen. "Trudy wants to know if you'd like more coffee," he said to Miss Conover.

Then he spotted the button. "Where did that come from?" he asked in surprise.

"Nan found it on the beach," Bert said. "Do you know whose it is?"

"Sure! It belongs to Slippery Jenks!"

CHAPTER III

GEORGE WASHINGTON'S HOUSE

"SLIPPERY JENKS!" Bert exclaimed. "Are you sure?"

"I'd know those silver buttons anywhere!" Toony insisted. "This one is his, all right!"

In reply to the children's questions, Toony explained that Slippery Jenks had been to Mexico some years before when he was working on a freighter. "He bought several hammered-silver buttons there and sewed the set on every jacket he's had since!"

"What does the design on it mean?" Nan asked curiously, fingering the button.

"It's an old design used by the Indians in Mexico," Tony replied. "It's the sun and rain. Slip is mighty proud of those buttons."

"What was he looking for in the bushes?" Freddie piped up.

Toony shook his head. "That I don't know," he answered, "but I can tell you he was probably up to no good!"

"Let's find out!" Flossie proposed eagerly.

"How?" Freddie demanded.

"We can go see Mr. Jenks and take his button to him!"

"Well—" Toony looked at Aunt Alice. "What do you think, ma'am?"

"I have some errands for you to do in River Edge," the elderly woman said, smiling. "The children could go with you."

"Hurray!" Freddie shouted joyfully.

A short time later the *White Gull* left Conover Island with Toony at the wheel. As soon as they reached the River Edge dock and Toony had tied up the launch, he said, "We'll go to Slip's house first."

He led the twins up a steep side street of the little river town and stopped at a shabby-looking one-story cottage. He rang the front door bell. There was no answer, nor any sign of life in the house.

"I guess Slip's not here," Toony said, but rang once more.

The children were turning away, disappointed, when the door to the next house opened. A thin woman with a sharp nose and frizzy blond hair came out onto the porch.

"No use ringin'," she told them. "Mr. Jenks isn't home much."

"Do you know where we could find him?" Bert asked politely.

The woman folded her arms and looked disapproving. "No, I don't," she replied. "All I know is he's been boastin' a lot lately. Says he's goin' to make his fortune. Don't know how he figures to do that in River Edge!"

"We have something that belongs to him!" Flossie piped up.

"Maybe you'll see him out on the river," the woman suggested. "He spends a lot of time in that boat of his!"

Toony thanked the talkative neighbor, and they left. Toony took care of Aunt Alice's errands in town, then the group boarded the *White Gull* and headed back to the island. They kept watch but saw no sign of Slippery Jenks or his boat.

The twins were not discouraged, however. "At least we have his button," Bert said. "That's one good clue."

"Maybe he'll come back looking for it," Nan added hopefully.

At luncheon Aunt Alice told the children, "I've invited the son of a friend of mine to come over this afternoon to meet you. His name is Cliff Myers—he's ten years old."

"Swell!" Bert exclaimed.

Early in the afternoon Cliff pulled up at the dock in a bright red rowboat. Bert ran down to meet the visitor. He was a stocky boy with curly black hair and a rather sullen look in his eyes.

"That's a neat boat you have!" Bert said admiringly as Cliff tied his craft to a post.

"She's the best on the Hudson River!" Cliff said boastfully.

Bert took the visitor up to the house and introduced him to his brother and sisters. Cliff looked from one twin to another. "Isn't it sort of spooky having someone look just like you?" he asked.

"Why no, we think it's fun," Nan replied. "Do you have any brothers or sisters?"

"Naw!" Cliff said rudely. "I'm an only child, and there's no one else like me in the whole world!"

Just then Aunt Alice brought several games out to the children, who settled down to play. Freddie told Cliff about the box which had disappeared from the dock.

"We're going to find it," Flossie added. "We like to find things for people."

"How are you going to find a silly old box?" Cliff scoffed. "You kids are kooky!"

At that moment Toony came out onto the

porch. "How would you children like to go down the river to Newburgh and visit Washington's house?" he asked.

"Washington's house?" Nan echoed in surprise.

Toony explained that General George Washington had made his headquarters in Newburgh for the last year of the Revolutionary War. "The house overlooks the river, and the museum has many interesting exhibits."

"I'll take you in my boat," Cliff said.

"Thanks, but Miss Conover wants me to use her launch," Toony said. "We'd be too many for your rowboat, I'm afraid."

Cliff scowled and shrugged his shoulders. He ran ahead and jumped into the *White Gull*. Taking his place as near the wheel as possible, he waited for the others. All the way down the river he gave Toony advice.

Toony heaved a sigh of relief when they reached the Newburgh dock and tied up. "Just follow me," he said, "and don't get lost."

He led the way up the steep streets of the town until they came to a large fenced-in area. In the center of a green lawn was a small fieldstone house with lovely shade trees. It had windows with many small panes of glass and a steeply slanting roof.

Toony motioned the twins and Cliff to go in

through the gate, then said, "A friend of mine lives on this street. I'd like to say hello to him. You children take a tour of the house and museum. I'll be back to meet you in a little while."

Inside the house, the children looked around with interest. Several of the rooms were furnished in the style of the Colonial period.

"Look at that huge chest!" Nan exclaimed, pointing to a wooden piece of furniture against one wall. It reached nearly to the ceiling and had carved posts at each end.

The woman in charge came forward. "That is called a *Kas,*" she explained. "It was brought from Holland by the early Dutch settlers."

Bert had wandered into the next room. "Come see this strange fireplace," he called.

It was not recessed like a fireplace. The logs were placed on a stone floor under a huge chimney. The wall back of it was also made of stone.

"It's called an open hearth fireplace," the guide told them.

While Bert and Nan were examining the fireplace, Cliff went back to the *Kas* to see if he could open the doors. Freddie and Flossie meantime walked out into the sunshine.

"Oh boy, a well!" Freddie cried, running over to a round stone structure. Above it hung a wooden bucket suspended from the end of a long wooden pole.

Flossie peered over the stone wall. "It isn't a well at all!" she said. "There's just ground in here!"

"I'm going to dip the bucket in it anyway!" Freddie declared.

The pole which held the bucket passed through a notched tree trunk and was held to the ground by a large stone. Freddie straddled the pole and pushed the stone aside with his foot. Up went the pole with Freddie!

"Help!" he cried. "Help!"

Quickly Flossie ran to her brother. She managed to grab his foot and pull him down.

"Thanks, Flossie," he exclaimed. "I guess I won't dip the bucket after all!" He shoved the stone back in place and anchored the end of the pole.

"I wonder what that is down by the river," Flossie remarked. She pointed to a large, square monument of stone on the bluff.

"Let's go look at it," Freddie proposed, and the small twins ran across the lawn.

"Oh," cried Flossie, "it's a little building!"

"And there's writing on it," said Freddie, squinting to read the words carved in stone. "This monument's for some soldiers who fought in the Revolutionary War," he told his sister.

The twins saw that there were large arched

Up went the pole with Freddie!

openings on all four sides of the monument. They were closed by iron gates. Freddie and Flossie peered through the bars. Inside was a square, empty room.

"Freddie," Flossie cried, "see those little stairs in the corners. I think they reach to the roof. Wouldn't it be fun to go up them?"

"But these gates are locked!" her twin said sadly. Then as he leaned against it, the gate moved!

"Come on, Flossie!" he said gleefully.

Quickly the twins pushed open the gate and ran into the room. Winding, open iron stairways rose at two corners. Freddie ran up one while Flossie scampered up the other. They met on the roof.

"Oh! Isn't it pretty?" Flossie exclaimed, as she looked at the broad river far below.

"I'll race you down!" Freddie proposed. "Last one's a monkey's uncle!"

With a giggle Flossie ran over to the stairway and started downward.

"We're supposed to begin together!" Freddie protested. But he took the steps two at a time and reached the bottom a second before Flossie. "I won!" he cried.

Seeing her twin reach the ground before she did, Flossie became excited and missed the last step. She tumbled in a heap on the floor!

"Are you hurt?" Freddie asked as he rushed over and helped her up.

"My knee!" Tears came to the little girl's eyes as she looked at her skinned knee.

"Don't cry, Flossie!" Freddie urged. "I'll bandage it!" He pulled a handkerchief from his pocket and wound it around his sister's knee. "There! Is that better?"

Flossie nodded, and a smile broke through her tears. "I'm not a monkey's uncle!"

Just then Nan's voice reached them. "Flossie! Freddie!" she called. "Where are you? We're going into the museum."

"We'd better go," Freddie said to his sister. "Can you walk okay?"

Flossie replied she was all right. Freddie took her hand, and the two ran across the lawn toward the museum. When they went in, the lobby was empty except for a sandy-haired man seated behind a desk.

He looked up from his book. "Are you Freddie and Flossie?" he asked.

When the twins said yes, he smiled. "I'm Mr. Watts, the caretaker here. Your sister asked me to tell you that she and the others are in the basement."

"Thank you," Flossie said.

At that moment a piercing shriek rang through the building!

CHAPTER IV

A NIGHTTIME ADVENTURE

THE startled twins looked at each other, then at the caretaker. "That scream came from the cellar! Something terrible's happened!" Flossie cried, and the twins, followed by Mr. Watts, hurried down the stairs.

Bert and Nan raced to meet them at the bottom of the steps.

"What's wrong?" the museum man demanded.

"It's Cliff!" Bert cried. "He's stuck! I can't get him loose!" Bert pointed.

Everyone looked at the far wall in amazement. Along it were two immense logs. At the end of one hung a huge iron chain.

Cliff was wedged fast in one of the big links!

"Help! Get me out of here!" the squirming boy yelled.

"Hold still!" Mr. Watts commanded, as they all ran over. The caretaker turned to Bert. "If you and your sister will grab the links and keep the chain steady, I'll see if I can pull your friend out!"

Bert and Nan took hold of the iron links and braced themselves while Mr. Watts got a firm grip on Cliff and pulled hard.

The boy's body moved slightly, but he cried, "Ow! You're hurting me!"

"Let out your breath, Cliff," Bert suggested. "That'll make you relax."

The chunky boy did so. This time Mr. Watts gave a powerful heave, and Cliff slid clear of the iron ring. He dropped to the floor.

"Are you hurt?" the museum man asked.

Cliff shook his head sheepishly.

"Now tell me how this happened," the care-taker said firmly.

Cliff shuffled his feet. "I just wanted to swing in one of those big links," he explained in a rush.

"Well, I guess now you know it wasn't such a smart idea," Mr. Watts said.

Bert and Nan were a little upset over Cliff's antics. "You'd better watch your step," Bert told the boy in a whisper, "or we'll all be asked to leave."

Cliff sneered and turned away. The older

twins looked at one another in disgust. Freddie and Flossie, however, were fascinated by the huge iron links and stood staring at them.

"This is part of the chain that was strung across the Hudson River in the Revolutionary War," Nan explained to them.

"Boy!" cried Freddie. "It's the biggest chain in the *world!*"

"It's the strongest, too," said Flossie, eyeing Cliff and grinning. Then, with a puzzled look, she asked, "Why would anyone put a chain across the river?"

Mr. Watts smiled as he told her, "The Americans wanted to keep the British ships from joining the rest of their forces in the north."

Bert had walked over to a case filled with small replicas of old vessels. "Come look at these ship models," he urged, and the others followed.

"Here are some Toony was telling us about on the way down!" Nan pointed out. "The *Henry Clay* and the *Mary Powell!*"

"Those old side-wheelers sure look funny now, don't they?" Bert remarked, staring at the huge paddle wheels at the center of each side of the ships. "But I'd like to have one of my own!"

After all the children had seen the rest of the displays, Nan said, "Why don't we go upstairs? Flossie and Freddie missed the things up there."

"Good idea," Bert agreed, and the group, led by Mr. Watts, climbed to the main floor. The caretaker took his place again at the desk, and the children trooped into a large room filled with exhibits.

"Oh boy!" cried Freddie. "Look at all the glass cases!" He eagerly flitted from one to another.

"Take it easy, Freddie," warned Bert. "We don't want any more accidents!"

Flossie giggled. "Freddie jumps around like the fleas in the flea circus!"

"Come see this display," Nan called to the younger twins.

The articles had been owned by General George Washington and his wife, Martha. There were yellowed documents, diaries, and old muskets.

"Ooh, look over there!" Flossie cried and ran to peer at some cases displaying worn, faded uniforms, women's lace-trimmed bonnets, and elaborate silk dresses.

Presently the children strolled out into the hall again. Mr. Watts smiled at them. "Would you like to go to the second floor and see the exhibits up there?" With a twinkle in his eye, he added, "I don't think you can get into any trouble, but just to make sure, I'll come along!"

The twins and Cliff followed him to the display rooms upstairs. As Nan walked toward one of the glass cases, she stopped short. In it was a doll dressed just the way Aunt Alice had described hers. Could it be the same one?

"Bert!" Nan cried. Her twin hurried over. "Look! Do you think this could be Aunt Alice's missing doll?"

"Let's ask Mr. Watts." Bert was excited, too.

When he heard the question, Mr. Watts shook his head. "I'm sorry to disappoint you, but that doll has been in the museum for several years. It was donated by a lady who lives here in Newburgh."

"Oh!" Nan said.

Bert told Mr. Watts the story of the disappearance of Aunt Alice's heirlooms.

"Too bad," the caretaker said. "If I hear of either of those things being offered for sale, I'll let you know."

At that moment Toony came up the stairs. "If you're ready," he said to the older twins, "we'd better start back."

Later, as he steered the *White Gull* up the river, Toony pointed to a mountain along the east bank. "That's Mount Beacon," he explained. "See that little line running up to the top?"

The children strained their eyes. "Yes—I do!" Freddie called out.

In the glass case was a doll dressed
just like Aunt Alice's

"That's what is called an inclined railroad," Toony continued. "It goes right up the mountain. Maybe we can ride on it."

"Oh boy! Let's!" Freddie said enthusiastically.

"Why is it called Mount Beacon?" Nan asked.

Toony said that during the Revolutionary War fires, or beacons, were lighted on top of the mountain. "It was part of a signal system the American Army used," he explained.

At the children's urging Toony told them some stories of the Hudson in the days when the old side-wheelers made their way up and down. "There's a rhyme that the old river men used to recite about the towns along the bank. Would you like to hear it?"

"Yes! Please!" the small twins cried.

Toony recited:

> "West Point and Middletown,
> Konnosook and Doodletown,
> Kakiak and Mamapaw,
> Stony Point and Haverstraw!"

The children laughed at the funny names. "Mamapaw, Papapaw!" Flossie sang, giggling.

"Let's all make up rhymes!" Nan said.

The others thought this would be fun, and

there was silence for a few minutes. Then Nan spoke up. "I have one!"

"Say it!" Freddie urged.

Nan cleared her throat and recited:

"New York, London, Paris, Rome
　But best of all I love my home—
　Good old Lakeport—that's my poem!"

They all cheered, then Bert recited:

"Flossie B skinned her knee,
　Freddie B jumps like a flea.
　They get in mischief, yessiree!
　But yippee! They're the kids for me!"

Freddie jumped up. "I'm a flea! I'm a flea!" he cried, and began to hop around.

"Here's our dock," Toony announced, grinning. "Sit down, flea, and avoid a shock!"

"Oh, Toony! You made a poem too!" Flossie cried in delight.

Toony laughed and made fast the launch. But Cliff snorted and did not join in the fun. After he had left in his rowboat, the twins dashed into the house to tell their mother and Aunt Alice about the day's adventures.

"I can see you're finding the Hudson River an exciting place!" said Aunt Alice, laughing.

"It's full of old things and new poetry," said Flossie.

When her aunt and mother looked puzzled, Nan and Bert recited their funny verses.

That evening, as Nan was getting ready for bed, she glanced out the window. The night was dark, and she could see little, but she heard small waves striking the rocky shore. Suddenly she leaned out over the sill excitedly and gazed toward the river. Two tiny lights were bobbing up and down on the water just off the side of the island!

"I wonder what they are?" Nan asked herself.

At that moment Flossie, already in bed, stirred. "Are you awake?" Nan asked softly.

"Yes," Flossie whispered.

"There's something funny out on the water," Nan said. "Come and see."

Flossie scurried out of bed and joined Nan at the window. "Where?" she asked.

Silently Nan pointed out the two bobbing lights. "What are they, Nan?" Flossie said in surprise.

"I don't know," Nan replied, "but I think we should find out. They may have something to do with the mystery! Let's call Bert."

"No, don't call him," Flossie objected with an impish grin. "Let's go out ourselves and see what the lights are. We'll tell Bert and Freddie in the morning for a surprise!"

Nan laughed. "All right!" she agreed. "That's what Bert and Freddie did to us when they almost caught that man! Maybe we can get ahead of them."

The girls hurried into their robes and slippers, tiptoed past the boys' room, and pattered down the stairs. Once outside, they stopped.

"If we saw the lights from our window," Nan reasoned, "they must be in the water off the south side of the island." She started in that direction.

Flossie followed. The next minute she whispered, "Nan! Something's standing there! It looks like an animal, but it isn't moving!"

Nan could just make out a shadowy figure in the dark. It certainly appeared to be an animal of some kind, but why didn't it run away?

Then she began to laugh. "Why, Flossie!" Nan said. "That's the iron dog!"

The girls made their way toward the water. They could no longer see the bobbing lights which were hidden by the shore line. But as they drew nearer the water, they heard the sound of oars.

"Someone's in a rowboat!" Nan whispered. "Maybe we can see who it is!" She stepped forward.

The next instant Nan stumbled and pitched headlong down the riverbank!

CHAPTER V

THE MOUNTAIN CHASE

"NAN!" Flossie screamed when her sister disappeared down the embankment. But Nan did not reply. There was only silence. The bobbing lights were gone. "Help!"

Flossie screamed again. "Help!"

The front door of the house flew open, and the four grownups ran out. Toony carried a flashlight. "Where are you?" he called.

"Here!" Flossie cried. "By the riverbank!"

"What happened, Flossie?" Mrs. Bobbsey asked anxiously as she hurried up.

"D-down there!" Flossie stammered, pointing. "Nan and I—we were going to see the lights and she—she fell over!"

Quickly Toony flashed his light on the bank. "There she is!" he cried. "I'll get her!"

By the time Toony had picked his way down the stony, steep slope, Nan was on her feet.

"You all right?" Toony asked with concern.

"I guess the breath was knocked out of me," Nan replied unsteadily. "But I don't think I'm hurt—just scratched."

Toony helped Nan scramble up over the rocks. By this time Bert and Freddie had come.

"Jeepers! What were you trying to do, Nan?" Bert asked in amazement.

"Let's go back into the house," Aunt Alice suggested. "Then we can hear the whole story."

A few minutes later they were all seated around the dining room table. Trudy brought in hot chocolate and a plate of cookies.

Bert and Freddie and the grownups listened with interest as Nan and Flossie described the bobbing lights and the sound of oars.

"What do you think the lights could be, Aunt Alice?" Mrs. Bobbsey asked curiously.

"Perhaps someone out night fishing," the elderly woman suggested.

"Well, whatever the lights were," said the twins' mother, "I want you girls to promise me not to go out alone at night again!"

Nan and Flossie quickly promised. On their way up to bed again, Bert said to Nan, "I don't think those lights belonged to any fisherman. Otherwise, why would they have gone out when you fell? A fisherman would have rowed to shore to help you!"

"Do you suppose it was Slippery Jenks again?" Nan ventured.

"Could be," Bert said in a puzzled tone, "but I can't figure out what he'd be doing near the island."

"I can't either, Bert. Well, see you in the morning."

At breakfast Mrs. Bobbsey said, "Aunt Alice and I are going to start packing some of her things today. She has suggested that Toony take you children over to Mount Beacon while we're working."

"That's great!" Bert exclaimed. "We saw it from the river yesterday."

"May we go up that little railroad?" Freddie asked hopefully.

His mother gave her consent. When the twins were ready for the trip, they ran down the path to the dock. Toony was waiting. "All aboard!" he said with a grin.

Later, out on the river, Nan looked around her and exclaimed, "It's really beautiful, with those mountains on both sides!"

Toony agreed. "There's a saying among the Hudson River folks that once a man has lived in the shadow of these mountains he'll never be the same again."

"Does that mean children, too?" Flossie asked. "I don't feel any different yet!"

"I don't think you'll change much!" Toony replied with a chuckle. Then he went on, "Did you know the Indians called the Hudson 'the stream that flows both ways'?"

"Why was that?" Bert asked with interest.

Toony explained that the source of the Hudson is a lake high up in the Adirondack Mountains called Tear of the Clouds. From this source, the river flows south, fed by many mountain streams as it moves along.

"But at the southern end," Toony went on, "it's really an arm of the sea. The ocean tide causes the river to flow north!"

The children laughed at the idea of a river which flowed both ways. By this time the launch was nearing the east bank.

"I see a dock where I can tie up," Toony said. "It won't be much of a walk to the station of the inclined railroad."

When he reached the dock, two men were just about to step into a motorboat. Bert nudged Nan. "See that man with gray hair?" he said. "Isn't that the Customs man, Mr. Ward?"

At that moment the man looked up and saw the children. "Hello there!" he called. "It's my little friends from the restaurant!" He said something to his companion, then walked over to the group.

"Have you found any smugglers?" Freddie asked after Nan had introduced the man to Toony and the small twins.

Mr. Ward looked worried. "No, I haven't," he admitted. "I came over today on a tip that a smuggler was around here, but I haven't been able to get any clues!"

"We'll let you know if we see anyone acting suspicious," Bert assured the man as the children said good-by and set off for the inclined railroad.

"Ooh! It looks steep!" Flossie cried, eyeing the narrow track which seemed to go almost straight up.

"It's the steepest in the world," Toony said proudly. "When you reach the top you'll have a seventy-five mile view!"

A little white car was waiting at the foot of the mountain. Several people were already seated on the gray wooden benches which ran across the width of the car. All were placed so that the passengers would be facing outward.

The twins settled onto the first bench, and in a few moments the little train started off with a jerk. It ran along on level ground for a short distance, then began the ascent.

"Ooh! It *is* steep!" Flossie exclaimed a minute later. She watched breathlessly as the ground seemed to drop away beneath her.

The track ran through thick woods, but far below, the Hudson valley lay stretched out before them. Bert put his hands down on the wooden seat and leaned back to enjoy the view. As he did so, his hand touched something. He picked up a piece of yellow paper which had been wedged between the slats of the bench.

Bert idly glanced at the paper. Then he poked Nan, who was seated next to him. "Look at this marked map!" he exclaimed.

Nan took the paper and studied it. "Oh, Bert, here's Mount Beacon marked with a cross. And this place could be Aunt Alice's island, with a cross marked right next to it!"

What could the cross mark mean? The map was passed on to Toony and the small twins, but they had no ideas about it.

"Another mystery," Bert declared, putting the paper in his pocket.

Presently the little car jerked to a stop at the top of the mountain. As everyone alighted, Freddie announced, "I'm hungry!"

"We can have lunch over there." Toony pointed out a large one-story building.

Inside, he and the twins lined up at the counter and ordered sandwiches and milk. When they had finished, Toony paid the bill and went over to speak to a man he knew. Nan and Bert examined some postcards on a rack while Freddie played with several tiny automobiles which were displayed on a table.

Flossie still sat at the counter. She had ordered a double-dip cone and was struggling to finish it before the ice cream melted.

"Cherry soda!" a man's harsh voice said to the girl behind the counter.

Flossie looked up at the man standing beside her. He was tall and thin and had shifty eyes. Suddenly she noticed the carved silver buttons on his jacket!

"Slippery Jenks!" she thought excitedly. "I must tell Toony!" She began to slide off the tall stool.

As she did, the man turned around. His elbow struck Flossie's arm. The ice cream flew out of the cone and landed on the front of his jacket!

"What—!" he yelled.

"I'm awf'ly sorry, Mr. Slip," Flossie gulped. The man glared at her, then turned and rushed from the building.

"Bert! Nan!" Flossie called as she ran toward them. "I just saw Slippery Jenks!"

Freddie and Toony heard her and ran up. "Where, Flossie?" Bert cried.

"He's got on his silver buttons—and I spilled my ice cream on him—and he ran away!"

The ice cream landed on the front of
his jacket

Finally Flossie calmed down enough to tell what had happened. "He ran out the door!" she concluded.

"Let's chase him!" Freddie said and dashed toward the entrance, the others close behind.

"There's Mr. Jenks!" Nan cried. The tall man was already some distance away, hurrying along a path which seemed to lead to a tall monument on the very top of the mountain.

"He's making for the Beacon monument!" Toony exclaimed. "It marks the place where the Revolutionary soldiers had their signal fires."

The man ahead apparently had no idea that he was being followed. He walked along among the low trees without looking back. The growth became thinner, and he began to scramble over rocks toward the monument.

"What shall we do?" Nan asked. "He's getting way ahead of us."

"Let's wait here and see what *he's* going to do," Bert suggested.

Toony and the children stationed themselves behind a clump of bushes and watched the man climb to the highest point of the mountain. Then he took something from his pocket. The next minute there was a flash of light. It went on and off several times.

"He's signaling someone!" Bert cried.

CHAPTER VI

A FUNNY HIDING PLACE

"JUST like the Revolutionary soldiers did!" Freddie exclaimed as he watched the man signaling from the mountain top.

"Toony, is that man really Slippery Jenks?" Nan asked seriously.

"I can't be sure," Toony replied. He looked worried. "I didn't see the fellow while he was in the restaurant, and he's too far away for me to identify."

"But he had fancy silver buttons on his jacket!" Flossie insisted.

"Were any of them missing?" Bert wanted to know. "Remember, he lost one when Freddie and I tackled him the other night."

Flossie squinted her eyes in deep thought, then admitted she had not noticed whether or not any buttons were gone from the man's coat.

"Come on!" Bert urged. "Let's go up and talk to him!"

Nan had been watching the figure by the monument. "He walked around the other side," she announced. "We'd better hurry!"

The children, followed by Toony, began to scramble over the rocks. In a few minutes they reached the monument, breathless. Freddie and Flossie dashed around to the far side.

"He isn't here!" they cried out.

The children looked around, baffled. Where had he gone?

Then Nan pointed down the mountain. A tall figure could be seen dodging in and out among the trees. "There he is! Can he go back to Beacon that way?" she asked Toony.

The river man shook his head. "No, he'll come out farther down the river."

"Say," Bert said excitedly, "do you suppose he came up in the train before we did and lost this map on the seat?"

"And didn't want to go back on the train because Flossie recognized him and he was afraid we'd ask him questions!" Nan cried.

"Maybe the girl at the lunch counter knows who he is," Flossie suggested.

"Good idea!" Bert exclaimed. "We'll ask her!"

They hurried back to the restaurant and up to the pretty young woman behind the counter. Flossie put her question.

"No, I don't know his name," the girl said, "but the man you describe comes in here several times a week. Never buys anything but a bottle of soda."

"We saw him go up to the monument," Bert went on. "But he went down the other side of the mountain."

"That's queer," the waitress said. "I've noticed he usually rides back on the railroad. But he always does walk over to the monument each time he's here."

A bell sounded, announcing that the train was ready to descend. The children thanked the girl and went with Toony to the car.

Again Bert and Nan sat beside each other. Bert pulled the map from his pocket. "Maybe we can find some clues," he suggested.

The twins studied the crude drawing from all angles. It seemed to cover the section of the river midway between New York City and Albany. Landmarks such as Stony Point, Storm King Mountain, and Mount Beacon were labeled in pencil. There were tiny crosses at Mount Beacon as well as the island farther up the river which the twins were certain belonged to Aunt Alice.

Nan sighed. "I can't make anything out of it. Can you, Bert?"

"No." Her twin looked discouraged.

"Wait a minute!" Nan exclaimed. "This cross at Aunt Alice's island is on the south side. That's where Flossie and I saw the queer bobbing lights!"

"Do you suppose there's a connection between the cross and the lights?" Bert asked.

"There might be, but what is it?" Nan said. "Do you think the man at the monument might have been signaling to someone on the island?"

"But there's no one on the island except Aunt Alice, Toony, and Trudy!" Bert objected.

By this time the little car had reached the bottom of the mountain. Toony and the children jumped out and walked to the dock. During the ride home they all discussed the mysterious map.

"Let's go look at the south side of the island now while it's daytime," Nan proposed.

After Toony had docked the boat and gone up to the house, the four twins ran to the rocky side of the little island. There were many low trees and bushes here, and the ground fell off sharply to the river.

"There's the place you went down, Nan!" Freddie said, pointing out a path in the dirt.

"Last night the lights were on the water just about here," Nan remarked, beginning to pick her way down the slope.

The others followed. At the bottom was a

narrow stretch of stony ground. The twins stood on this and peered carefully into the water. Small pieces of wood floated past, but that was all.

"I guess what Flossie and I saw last night is gone by this time," Nan said finally.

When the twins walked into the house, they found Mrs. Bobbsey and Aunt Alice busy sorting china and glassware. Flossie saw a tiny blue and white tea set with cups not more than an inch high and two inches across.

"How darling!" she exclaimed, picking up the dainty teapot. "Was it yours when you were little, Aunt Alice?"

Miss Conover smiled. "Yes," she replied, "and I'm saving it for another little girl."

"Oh!" Flossie's eyes widened hopefully.

But Aunt Alice said nothing more, and Freddie began to tell about the inclined railroad. Quietly Flossie put down the teapot.

When Freddie had finished, Mrs. Bobbsey said, "My! You not only had a good time, but an adventure, too!" She smiled. "We had an unexpected visitor while you were gone."

"Who?" the twins chorused.

"A police officer came to talk to Aunt Alice about the box which disappeared."

"Has he found any clues?" Bert asked.

"The officer thinks that if the box was stolen,

the doll and the flute may turn up in one of the antique shops around this section," Aunt Alice explained.

"Oh, couldn't we go to some of them and look for your things?" Nan asked excitedly.

Miss Conover thought this over for a moment. "Perhaps, we could, Nan," she said. "It might be a very good idea. Mrs. Myers has always urged me to use her car when I needed one. I'll call her."

After Aunt Alice returned from the telephone she said it had been arranged that they would borrow Mrs. Myers' car the next day.

"I hope Cliff won't go with us!" Flossie whispered to Freddie. "He's a pain!"

Toony took Miss Conover and the Bobbseys to River Edge in the morning and said he would await their return. Mrs. Myers welcomed the visitors warmly at her home. She was a small, friendly woman with curly dark hair. She said her son was spending the day with a friend. "He'll be sorry to miss you," she added.

The twins were relieved. While the grownups were talking, Flossie said to Freddie, "I like her better than I do Cliff!"

When Aunt Alice explained that she and the Bobbseys were going to search for her missing heirlooms, Mrs. Myers was very much interested.

"My neighbor was called to New York City yesterday," she said. "I promised to stay with her elderly mother this week so you're welcome to take my car any day."

"Wonderful!" said Aunt Alice. "Thank you."

The country around River Edge, the twins learned, had many shops that specialized in early American furniture, household utensils, old tools, and bric-a-brac. With Mrs. Bobbsey driving, they went along a country road until they came to a rambling farmhouse. Across the front of the large red barn behind it was a sign: *Hickory Hill Antiques.*

A pleasant-looking woman welcomed them and listened with interest to their queries about Miss Conover's fashion doll and flute. The shop owner shook her head—she had seen neither.

While Aunt Alice and Mrs. Bobbsey continued to discuss antiques with the woman, the twins wandered about the barn looking at the various articles for sale. There were old carriage lamps, metal molds used for making candles, and long-handled covered pans. A sign said they were bed warmers!

Bert examined some ancient muskets, and Nan looked over a pile of old maps. Freddie and Flossie started a game of hide-and-seek.

"You look out the door and count to ten," Flossie directed, "then try to find me."

When Freddie turned around, Flossie had disappeared. Her twin walked about the large room looking behind chests and under tables. As he passed a large covered box which stood on legs, he heard a stifled giggle.

Quickly Freddie flung up the top of the chest. "I caught you!" he cried.

Flossie climbed out and smoothed her skirt. "All right," she said. "Now I'll count and you hide!" She covered her eyes and began, "One —two—three—"

At the count of ten she looked around. There was no sign of her twin. Softly Flossie crept around the shop. In one corner stood a large grandfather's clock.

As she passed it, Flossie thought she heard a faint clanging noise. She stopped short and stared at the grandfather's clock. A big grin came over her face. "I'll bet I know who's in there!" she told herself.

Flossie put her hand on the knob of the clock's big front door and gave it a tug. The door burst open and Freddie came tumbling out, knocking over his twin. The two children shrieked with laughter.

"How'd you know I was in there?" Freddie asked, getting up and brushing himself off.

Freddie came tumbling out, knocking over
his twin

"Oh, I'm a hide-and-seek de-tective!" Flossie replied.

Just then Mrs. Bobbsey called from the door, "Come on, children! We're leaving now."

Freddie and Flossie joined the others. "Are we going to hunt some more for the dolly?" Flossie asked her mother.

"Yes, dear."

The friendly owner suggested several antique shops where they might look. The Bobbseys and Aunt Alice thanked her and said good-by.

After stopping at a country inn for lunch, they visited the other places. But no one had seen the old doll or the flute. Finally, there was only one shop left on the list.

"We'll go there, then I think we'll have to give up for today," Aunt Alice said.

A short time later Mrs. Bobbsey drew up before a small white house on the main street of a little town. A tiny white-haired woman opened the door and invited them in.

Aunt Alice asked about her fashion doll, but the woman said, "I haven't had one for years. They are not very common around here."

"Have you an old wooden flute?" Bert asked.

The shop owner brightened. "Yes, I have," she answered. "I bought one from a man just yesterday. I'll get it for you!"

CHAPTER VII

THE MUSHROOM CAVE

THE woman had an old flute! It *must* be Aunt Alice's, the twins thought.

Five minutes later the shop owner returned, carrying a wooden flute trimmed with silver.

Aunt Alice held out her hand. "It does look like mine!" she cried happily.

The twins held their breaths while she examined the slender musical instrument. Then Miss Conover shook her head disappointedly.

"This isn't mine! The flute I loaned to the museum had the initials J. C. carved on it. The original owner's name was Joost Conover."

"Joost!" Mrs. Bobbsey remarked. "That's an unusual name!"

"Joost is Dutch for George," her aunt said.

The children were so discouraged at the failure of their search that they were silent during the ride back to River Edge. As they drove down the main street, Toony came out of a barbershop. When he saw the car, he hailed them.

Mrs. Bobbsey drew up to the curb. "I have some news about Jenks," Toony announced.

"What is it?" the twins chorused.

Toony said he had discovered that Slippery was working in a mushroom cave not far from Kingston.

"Can we go there?" Bert asked eagerly.

"I guess so, if we can borrow Mrs. Myers' car," his aunt replied. "I'll ask her." Then she said to Toony, "We'll meet you at the dock in a little while," and they drove away.

Cliff was at home when they reached Mrs. Myers' house. Mrs. Bobbsey smiled at the boy. "We'd like to use your mother's car again tomorrow. Perhaps you can join us on that trip."

Mrs. Myers willingly offered her automobile, so it was agreed that Toony and the children would return the next morning. Aunt Alice and Mrs. Bobbsey would continue the packing.

On the way back in the launch Nan asked, "What *are* mushroom caves, Toony?"

The river man explained that a great deal of limestone rock had formerly been mined in the hills around Kingston. When the work had stopped, great caves had been left where the rock had been taken out.

"The dampness and the temperature of the caves are just right for growing mushrooms," he went on, "so some of the caves are used for that purpose nowadays."

"Ooh! I love caves!" Flossie exclaimed.

The next morning when the twins climbed into the *White Gull* again, Freddie noticed a large wicker basket on the seat next to Toony.

"What's that?" he asked curiously.

"Our lunch, my lad," Toony replied. "Trudy was afraid you'd starve, I guess!"

Freddie grinned. "We won't now!"

When they reached the Myers' house the car was parked at the curb and Cliff was waiting impatiently in the front seat. Mrs. Myers waved from a living-room window as Toony took the wheel and the Bobbsey twins piled in.

"Where is the cave?" Bert asked as they started off.

Toony said his friend did not know just which mushroom cave Slippery worked in. "There are some south of Kingston," Toony said. "I thought we'd look in those first."

Half an hour later Toony turned to the left off the main route onto a narrow country road. Steep hills rose on one side, while on the other was a swift-flowing stream.

Toony drove slowly, peering at the hills as he went along. "I'm looking for a cave," he explained. "Keep your eyes open. It'll probably look like a garage door built against the side of a mountain."

Suddenly Freddie called out, "I see one!"

The river man put on the brakes. A flat, rocky wall flanked by a large wooden door appeared at the base of the hill.

"I think you're right, Freddie," Toony said, as he turned off the road and parked. "We'll see if anyone's working in this cave."

He took a flashlight from his pocket and led the way toward the cave. "There aren't any tire marks leading to the entrance," he noted.

"No footprints, either," Bert observed.

"It's still worth investigating," Toony said, as he pulled open the huge door. It creaked and groaned, revealing a cavern so inky black that the flashlight beam could not pierce its depths. Fortunately, however, the light from the entrance enabled them to distinguish the area directly in front of them.

The children looked around, and Flossie grabbed Nan's hand. "It's spooky!" she said.

The damp, musty cave was as tall as a three-story building. From the rocky top and sides came the steady *drip, drip, drip* of water.

Bert ventured a short ways to one side, then stopped quickly. "Say!" he called, "there's a regular lake here!"

Toony beamed his flash onto the pool. From the sound of the water, it traveled a good distance along the inside of the cave, but the inadequate light gave no clue.

"We just can't see enough to walk any farther," said Toony. "Anyhow, there doesn't seem to be a soul in here—no noise, no prints. We'll have to try another cave."

As they stepped out into the sunlight again Flossie shivered. "I'm glad we didn't find the bad man in there."

They stopped to investigate several more caves in the area, but all proved to be empty. Finally they turned into a gasoline station, and Toony questioned the attendant.

"There's a cave just the other side of Kingston," the young man said. "I think a mushroom grower is using it."

Finally, at the bottom of a steep hill, Bert spotted the cave. This one also had a wooden door over the entrance, but it stood open. Toony and the children walked in.

"Ooh! It looks different from the others!" Flossie exclaimed. "Much nicer."

This time electric lights were strung along one side, but in the cave they gave off an eerie glow. Water dripped from the high ceiling, and the ground was covered with mud.

Squish, squish, squish! The children's shoes

squeaked as they walked through the soft muck. There was no other sound except that of the dripping water.

"Hello! Anyone around?" Toony called. There was no answer.

"Someone *has* been in here," Bert said, pointing to tire marks in the mud.

The passage through the cave was a winding one, so it was impossible to see very far ahead. On each side, where the dim electric lights did not penetrate, the children could barely make out openings in the rock walls.

"It seems to be empty," Toony said.

"Let's go around that next turn," Bert urged.

When they rounded the bend, they all stopped in astonishment. The cave had widened and now sloped downward into a great circle. The children saw several trucks parked around the walls and four or five small tractors moving busily about. Men were piling flat wooden trays on racks which were scattered in piles on the ground.

"Hello!" Toony called again.

A man driving one of the tractors shut off the motor and came up to the group. "Can I help you?" he asked pleasantly, surprised to see the visitors. "I'm the foreman."

Before Toony could answer, Flossie spoke up. "Where are all the mushrooms?" she asked.

The man waved his hand toward the racks of trays. "There they are," he said. "You can't see them now, but in about two weeks they'll pop up and cover those trays."

"Are the little seeds planted in them?" Nan asked.

The foreman explained that mushrooms did not grow from seeds, but from little bits called spores which came from the underpart of the mushroom cap. "We plant the spores in the straw mixture in the trays and—well, that's the way mushrooms are grown."

The foreman lifted out a tray for the children to see. At the same time Freddie happened to look over at a group of workmen near a rack. As he did, one of the men gave the visitors a startled glance and walked quickly toward a passage leading out from the large cave in the opposite direction.

"Maybe that's Slippery!" Freddie thought. He turned to Cliff, who stood next to him. "I'm going to follow that man!" he whispered.

"Okay! I'll come with you!" Cliff said.

Toony and the other twins were intent on the foreman's explanation about the mushroom tray and did not notice the two boys slip away. Freddie, in the lead, entered the dark passage. The man he had seen leave the work space was just disappearing around a corner.

Freddie ran after him. For a time he could keep the man in sight. Then the light grew dimmer, until, in another minute, Freddie found himself in complete darkness.

"Cl—iff," he said shakily, "are you here?"

There was no reply. Freddie turned around. He was alone in the black cave! Cliff had de-

serted him! The little boy was frightened. What should he do?

"I—I can't even see," he told himself. "Which way do I go?"

Bravely Freddie tried to be calm. He strained his eyes in the gloom. Then he saw a point of light in the distance and heard Nan calling, "Freddie! Freddie!"

"Here I am!" he cried happily and began to run back toward his sister. "I almost caught the bad man."

"What a shame you didn't!"

When they joined the others, Toony looked stern. "You must stay with us, Freddie," he said. "It's very easy to get lost in these caves, and we might not be able to find you. And, Cliff, you should not have left Freddie alone in there!"

Cliff's face grew red and he looked down at the ground. Freddie promised not to run away again. "But I thought I could catch Slippery!" he added, telling of his suspicions.

"That's what we wanted to ask you," Bert said to the foreman. "Does a man named Slippery Jenks work here?"

The foreman looked around. "Yes, but I don't see him. If it was Slip whom Freddie saw going down the tunnel, he probably went out another exit. It's possible to walk through these caves for miles if you know your way."

"Where can we catch him?" Bert demanded.

"I don't know. If I send you to one place, he'll probably come out another."

"We'll come back," Bert declared.

"I don't think Slippery will return if he's trying to avoid you," the foreman said, and Toony agreed.

Freddie felt bad, but said bravely, "I'll catch him some other way!"

The disappointed twins thanked the mushroom man, and all went back to the car. Toony drove on for a short distance, then turned into a picnic area.

"Maybe things will look brighter if we see what Trudy has for us to eat," he announced.

The wicker basket was filled with delicious sandwiches, fruit, and a chocolate cake. Toony and the children ate everything.

Finally Flossie asked, "Where shall we go now?"

"Would you like to see some animals?" Toony asked. "We're not far from the Catskill Game Farm."

"Oh, yes!" Freddie agreed enthusiastically.

The road to the game farm ran through a forest for much of the way. Then they drove into a clearing where many cars were parked. When the children and Toony had bought their tickets and walked inside the game area, Flossie saw a booth where various souvenirs were being sold.

"I want one of those funny hats!" she cried.

Bert pulled a bill from his pocket. "I'll treat you all to hats," he offered.

The hats were of different colors, and each one had a little white pompon on top. Flossie picked a green one, Nan a pink, while the boys chose brown.

Toony walked on with Nan, Freddie, and Cliff. Flossie stood by a fenced-off area to wait for Bert, who was getting his change. As her brother turned away from the booth, a look of alarm came over his face.

"Look out, Flossie!" he yelled.

CHAPTER VIII

A HUNGRY GIRAFFE

FLOSSIE jumped. The next instant she felt her hat being lifted from her head! "Why— why!" she stammered. Staring upward, she saw a calm-looking giraffe. In his mouth far above her head, he held Flossie's green hat!

The other children ran back and all stood laughing at the sight of the giraffe with Flossie's hat.

"Oh, please, Mr. Giraffe," Flossie begged, gazing at him, "give me back my hat! *Please* don't eat it!"

The funny, long-necked animal seemed to consider her words, then he leaned down and dropped the hat on Cliff's head!

The boy beamed. "See, he likes me!" he bragged. "Here, boy," he said, "take this!" Cliff held up an empty popcorn box.

"Don't give him that, Cliff!" Nan pleaded. "He'll eat it and make himself sick!"

But Cliff paid no attention. The giraffe grabbed the paper box and began to chew. At that moment an attendant rushed up with a long pole. Skillfully he hooked the pole in the box and pulled it away.

He looked sternly at Cliff. "A giraffe can't digest a paper box any better than you can!"

Toony apologized for the boy's mischief as Cliff shrugged his shoulders and walked away. The children went on past more enclosures containing different kinds of animals. They saw camels, zebras, bears, and a baby elephant.

Finally they reached an area where animals were roaming about among the visitors. Flossie picked up a little fawn and cuddled the creature in her arms.

"Isn't it darling?" she cried happily. The fawn nuzzled her face affectionately.

A little later Toony spoke up reluctantly, "It's getting late. We must start back."

"All right," Bert agreed. "But where's Cliff?"

They looked around. The boy was nowhere in sight. "I'll find him," Bert volunteered. "You all go on. We'll meet you at the car."

Toony, Nan, and the small twins walked toward the parking lot while Bert turned back. He went along and finally spotted Cliff.

The boy was backed up against a fence. He

looked terrified. Close in front of him stood a white llama, its jaws moving from side to side as it chewed. Each time Cliff tried to edge away from the fence, the llama followed him, still chewing steadily.

"Get me out!" Cliff cried when he saw Bert. "This crazy animal won't let me go!"

Bert walked over, put his hand on the llama's long neck, and gently coaxed him away. Cliff ran out to the walk.

"We're going home," Bert said when he caught up to the boy. "Toony's waiting for us at the car. Come on."

"I wasn't scared of that llama!" Cliff insisted. "But they're so fussy about their old animals here, I didn't want to touch him!"

"Okay, Cliff," Bert said good-naturedly.

Driving out to the highway again, the children heard the low rumble of thunder in the distance. "Is it going to rain?" Nan asked in surprise, looking up at the blue sky.

Toony chuckled. "I guess it's Rip Van Winkle's little men playing ninepins over the Catskill Mountains!"

"Who's Rip Van Winkle?" Freddie asked.

"He's a man in a story by Washington Irving, who wrote about people in this part of the country," Toony explained. "Rip slept for twenty years!"

"Wow!" Freddie exclaimed. "He must have been real sleepy!"

In response to the children's pleading, the river man told them the tale of Rip Van Winkle, who was resting under a tree one day and met a little man in old-time Dutch clothes. He led Rip up into the mountains to a place where a group of odd-looking men were playing ninepins. Rip drank some strange brew from a keg which the little men offered him. Then he fell asleep.

"When Rip woke up," Toony continued, "he had a long white beard. He made his way back to his village. Everything had changed, and Rip learned that he had been asleep for twenty years! So whenever we hear thunder in these mountains, we say it's the little men playing ninepins!"

"It's a neat story!" Freddie remarked, and the others agreed.

That night before they went to bed, the twins made a circle of the island, hoping to spot the mysterious bobbing lights, but none appeared.

"Maybe we scared away whoever it was," said Nan.

Aunt Alice phoned the police, but they had no news about her missing package. "I hope it will be found before I leave here," she said.

Then she added, "The Bobbsey twins are working hard on the case."

"Good for them!" said the captain.

The next morning Toony and Trudy were busy carrying trunks down from the attic. The children helped with the packing for a while, then Aunt Alice said to them, "Why don't you try some fishing? The Hudson River's a good place for that. Toony will find you some poles."

"We brought our own, thanks, Aunt Alice," Bert spoke up.

Presently the four children left the house with their fishing gear. "Where shall we try first?" Nan asked.

"Let's go to the south side of the island," Bert suggested. "We can sit on the bank and fish from there."

The four Bobbseys trooped to the spot.

"I'll go dig for worms," Freddie offered, running to a place where the earth was damp. Soon he had a good supply of earthworms.

The group settled down with their legs hanging over the edge of the slope and cast their lines out into the water below. In a few minutes Bert cried, "I have a bite!"

He began to reel in his line, but it came very slowly. "Boy! This is heavy!" Bert exclaimed. "I must have hooked a whale!"

"I'll help you," Freddie said. "I'm strong!"

At that moment Bert's catch came to the surface of the water. "It's only an old box!" Freddie cried. Everyone burst into laughter.

"But what a queer box!" Bert exclaimed.

Caught on the hook was a small metal drum.

Bert again reeled in his line. But just as the drum reached the bank, it slipped off the hook and sank back into the water.

"I'm going to try to get it!" Bert cried. He dashed to the house and returned in his swimming trunks. He scrambled down the bank and dived into the river.

The others watched breathlessly as he swam around under water. In a few seconds he came up. "No luck!" he said as he climbed the slope again. "I guess the mysterious box is gone!"

Suddenly Flossie cried out, "There's something on my line!"

"Maybe you've hooked the box, too!" Freddie said in excitement.

"But it's wiggling!" Flossie exclaimed as she struggled to hold her pole.

Bert rushed to her assistance. He skillfully reeled in the line, let it out, and pulled it in again until finally a big bass flopped onto the ground beside Flossie.

"I caught a fish! I caught a fish!" She jumped up and down in glee.

The twins fished awhile longer but without success. Finally they carried Flossie's bass into the kitchen. Toony was there.

"How'd you like to cook your fish for lunch?" he asked. "You could build a fire out on the rocks."

"Oh, yes!" Flossie agreed. "Let's do it!"

While Toony cleaned the bass, Trudy brought out a frying pan. She also provided bread, butter, tomatoes, and potato chips.

"This is going to be a good picnic!" Freddie exclaimed. "Won't you eat with us, Toony?"

The river man beamed. "Thank you," he said. "There's nothing I like better than a bass right out of the river cooked over an open fire!"

He helped build the fire, and soon it was crackling on the top of a big rock. The fish, when done, was flaky and delicious.

"You caught a very good fish, Flossie!" Toony said teasingly.

"Bert caught a funny one!" the little girl replied. "But it got away."

After Bert had told about the strange-looking metal drum he had hooked that morning, Toony nodded. "We find some queer things in the river," he observed. "Maybe that drum fell off a barge."

"I like the Hudson River," Freddie spoke up as he gazed out over the water. "There're always lots of boats on it."

"Yes, it's a mighty busy river," Toony agreed. "Freighters all the way from Europe go up it as far as Albany. The barges carry sand, cement, bricks, and oil."

"I'd like to know what was in that metal

drum," Bert mused. "It's probably at the bottom of the river now."

"Don't give up hope," said Toony.

Later that afternoon the twins brought out a jigsaw puzzle to the porch. As Bert emptied the pieces onto a table, Nan picked up the lid of the puzzle box. "It's a picture of a Hudson River boat!" she exclaimed.

They sorted out the pieces, and soon all four were bent over the table trying to fit the parts together. They worked silently for a while, absorbed in the puzzle.

Then Flossie spoke up. "Can you find a piece for the smokestack, Freddie?"

When there was no answer, Flossie looked up. "Where's Freddie?" she asked in surprise. None of them had noticed the little boy leave the table.

"Freddie! Freddie!" Flossie called and ran into the house. In a few minutes she was back. "I can't find Freddie anywhere!" she cried.

CHAPTER IX

SPOOKY LIGHTS

"FREDDIE missing!" Nan repeated. "But he must be around here somewhere. Did you look all through the house?"

"Yes!" Flossie said, her big eyes filling with tears. "He isn't there! He's lost!"

"He can't get off the island," Nan consoled her. "We'll find him."

Bert, Nan, and Flossie walked around the grounds calling Freddie as they went. No answer came. They searched beneath all the shrubbery and even looked up into the trees in case the little boy was hiding there.

When they neared the rocky side of the island, Nan grabbed Bert's arm. "You don't suppose he fell off the bank into the water!"

"We'll look, but you know Freddie can swim," Bert said reassuringly.

"Maybe he's trying to find that queer box you hooked this morning," Flossie suggested.

Bert slid down the steep embankment and looked around carefully. "I'm sure Freddie hasn't been here," he said finally.

Bert joined the girls again, and the three went to the other side of the island to examine the sandy beach. But they found no signs that anyone had been there. Finally Bert and his sisters came out onto the lawn in front of the house.

"I can't imagine where Freddie is!" Nan said in despair.

Suddenly her eyes lit on the cupola at the top of the old house. "I have an idea!" she cried and ran into the house.

Bert and Flossie followed. When they reached the hall, Nan was already dashing up the winding stairs which rose all the way through the center of the house.

"I'll be down in a minute!" she called back.

When Nan reached the top of the stairs she pushed open the door which led into the cupola room. There on the floor lay Freddie, fast asleep.

"Freddie!" Nan called. "Wake up! We've been looking all over for you."

The little boy sat up and rubbed his eyes.

"Oh, Nan!" he said in surprise. "How did you find me? I was playing Rip Van Winkle, and I went to sleep!"

Nan rumpled her small brother's hair. "Well, next time, please tell us before you vanish just where you're going!"

She and Freddie went downstairs to where Bert and Flossie were waiting and explained what had happened.

Flossie giggled. "You don't look as if you'd been asleep for twenty years, Freddie! Your hair isn't even white! And I'm glad we didn't have to hunt for you that long!"

At that moment Toony came out of the kitchen. "I'm going over to River Edge for groceries," he said. "Anyone want to come along? Miss Conover says it's all right if you want to go."

"Oh, yes!" the twins replied.

"Let's do some detective work while we're there," Bert suggested. "We can see if Mr. Jenks is home."

They jumped into the boat, and a short time later Toony pulled up to the River Edge dock. "I'll meet you back here in half an hour," he said.

While he set off for the supermarket, the children started up the street where Slippery Jenks lived. Again no one answered when they knocked on the door of the cottage.

As they turned away, the gossipy woman next door came out onto her porch. "Mr. Jenks is hardly ever at home in the daytime," she volunteered. "He's got a new boat."

The woman sniffed, then went on, "Don't know where he got the money to buy it. Couldn't make that much workin' with mushrooms!"

"Thank you," said Nan. "We'll come back some other time."

But the woman was not to be stopped. "Mighty queer goin's on over there," she continued. "I've seen Mr. Jenks sneak into his house at night, always carryin' somethin'." With that she went inside and shut the door.

"I'll bet Slip got some of the money to buy his boat by selling Aunt Alice's museum things!" Nan declared.

"Of course, we don't *know* that he stole the box," Bert reminded her.

Freddie spoke up excitedly, "Let's look in his windows. Maybe we can see what he brings home at night!"

The four children walked around the cottage peering in the windows. They saw nothing unusual.

"We may as well give up," Bert finally remarked and started down the street with Nan. They had gone only a few steps when they saw a tall, thin man walking toward them.

"I'm sure he's Slippery!" Bert whispered.

"He looks like the person we saw at Mount Beacon," Nan agreed. They stopped in front of the man, and Bert said, "Mr. Jenks—"

The man scowled, pushed Bert roughly aside, and went on. Freddie and Flossie were still at the side of the porch looking in the basement windows. When the man reached the house and turned into the path, he caught sight of the small twins.

"What are you doing here?" he yelled. "Get off my property!"

Freddie and Flossie jumped at the sound of the angry voice. Then they ran out of the yard to the spot where Bert and Nan were waiting.

"Let's get Toony," Nan urged. "Maybe Slippery will talk to him."

The children ran down the street. Toony was just coming out of the supermarket, his arms loaded with packages. He listened to Bert's story.

"Okay," he said. "I'll put these things in the boat, then we'll go up to Slip's place. Maybe I can get something out of the fellow."

But when they reached the house and Toony announced his presence, Slippery refused to open the door. "Go away!" he shouted. "I haven't anything to say to you, Staats!"

"We found your silver button, Slippery!"

"Get off my property!" he yelled

Toony called. "I want to know what you were doing on Miss Conover's island!"

"I was looking for my fishing pole!" Slippery said defiantly.

"A likely story!" Toony replied with scorn.

"I lost one off my boat," Slippery went on, "and thought it might have drifted onto the island. I wasn't doing any harm. There was no reason for those kids to jump me!"

"Well, I'm telling you to stay off that island!" Toony warned sternly as he motioned the twins to follow him down the street.

"Why didn't you ask him about the box?" Freddie wanted to know.

"He'd only say he hadn't taken it," Toony replied.

"That's right," Bert agreed. "We'll have to find some evidence before we can accuse him of stealing the box."

"It's funny he didn't ask for his button," Nan remarked. "I wonder if he was afraid to."

Although sorry that they had found no clue to Aunt Alice's missing heirlooms, the children talked excitedly about the mystery on the way back to the island.

That night as Nan was getting ready for bed, she glanced out the window which faced south. Something caught her attention, and she looked more carefully. Two lights bobbed just offshore!

"Flossie!" she called. "The lights are there again! Let's get the boys."

Hurriedly they put on robes and slippers, then tapped on the door of Bert and Freddie's bedroom and told them to come along.

"Oh boy! The lights are back!" Freddie exclaimed. "Let's find 'em!"

He and Bert led the way downstairs. The twins crept toward the front door. As they passed the living room, they saw their mother and Aunt Alice watching television and told them where they were going.

"Okay, but be careful," Mrs. Bobbsey said.

The children approached the bank on the rocky side of the island with caution. The two lights were not far from shore. They seemed to be attached to something which moved up and down with the ripples in the water.

"How can we get to them?" Nan asked. "It's too deep to wade out."

"I have an idea," Bert whispered. "Wait here for me, and don't make any noise." He crept away in the darkness.

In a few minutes he returned carrying a pole with a hook at the end of it. "I noticed this on the dock the other day," he whispered.

"I hope it will reach the lights," Nan replied eagerly.

Bert grasped the pole near the end and stretched out on the ground. He wriggled as close to the edge of the bank as he dared and held the pole over the water.

"I—think I—can—make it!" he panted.

"Be careful!" Flossie cried fearfully.

"Freddie and I will hold you," Nan told her twin.

They gripped Bert's legs firmly as he strained to reach the lights with the pole. Finally he got the hook around one of them and began to pull the light toward shore.

"It's attached to something!" Bert said triumphantly.

When it reached the narrow strip of beach, Bert stopped pulling. "Here, take the pole, Freddie," he directed. "I'm going down to see what's holding this light."

As silently as possible he slid down the rocky slope. By this time the light had gone out. Bert pulled a flashlight from his pocket and carefully beamed it over the ground until he located the object. There was a lantern attached to the top of a small metal cylinder, like a midget oil drum. Quickly he picked up the container and scrambled to the top of the bank.

"It's a drum just like the one I hooked

this morning!" he told the others, his voice shaking with excitement.

"Look! The second light!" Nan pointed to the water.

At the same moment everyone heard the sound of oars. The light disappeared. "Some-one has picked up another drum!" Bert whis-pered and played his light over the water. But its range was too short. The twins could see nothing.

"Let's take the drum to the house and see what's in it!" Freddie spoke up impatiently.

When the four children burst into the living room, Mrs. Bobbsey and Aunt Alice looked up at the object in amazement.

"We caught the light!" Flossie cried.

"Come on!" Freddie urged. "Open the drum!"

Bert ran to get Toony, and in a few minutes the river man came with some tools. In no time at all he had the metal drum open. The group huddled close, staring in surprise.

CHAPTER X

THE DRUM'S SECRET

BERT quickly tipped up the drum, and out poured a number of small boxes. Eagerly he took the top off one of the boxes. It was full of tiny pieces of metal!

"What are they?" Freddie asked in amazement.

Aunt Alice picked up one of the pieces—a tiny wheel. "Bring me that magnifying glass on the desk, please, Freddie," she said.

The little boy gave her the glass, and she held it over the wheel. "This says Swiss," she reported. "I think these are parts for watches."

"We ought to notify the police," Bert suggested.

Aunt Alice made the call, and within half an hour a police launch pulled up to the dock. An officer, who introduced himself as Lieutenant Daly, came to the house.

"I understand you've found a mysterious drum in the river," he said to Bert.

"Yes, and another one was picked up by somebody in a rowboat. We couldn't see him."

Bert led the officer over to the table where the tiny metal parts were spread out. "They're Swiss watch movements, all right!" the officer exclaimed. He opened several other small boxes. "Same thing here."

"But why were they floating on the river in the queer drum?" Nan wanted to know.

"That's what we'll have to find out," the officer said. "They may have fallen off a boat by accident or—there may be something illegal about these containers."

Lieutenant Daly examined the metal drum. "This lighting rig makes me think there's something crooked going on!"

Bert had an idea. "Do you think the parts were being smuggled into the country?"

"Could be. We'll check into it."

Bert told the police officer about Mr. Ward, the United States Customs Service man, and his search for smugglers on the Hudson River. "I have his phone number. Shall I call him?"

"Sure, go ahead!" Lieutenant Daly agreed. "I'll talk to him, too."

When Bert reached Mr. Ward, the Customs man was very interested. "Good for you, Bert!"

he exclaimed. "This discovery will be a big help to me. That drum does sound suspicious. I'll be over to the island early tomorrow morning." Then after a few words with the police officer he hung up.

Mr. Ward arrived early. After being introduced to Mrs. Bobbsey and Miss Conover, he examined the drum and the boxes of parts.

"We do know watch movements are being smuggled into the country," he said. "I'll take these parts along with me and check to see if the duty on them was paid."

"But how did they get in the river, and who put a light on the drum?" Freddie asked.

"It's a very clever trick," Mr. Ward explained. "This drum is specially constructed. There is a chemical in it. When the drum is thrown into the river and water enters it, the water turns the chemical into gas. This sends the drum to the surface and a mechanism inside lights the gas to act as a signal!"

"That sounds complicated!" Bert exclaimed.

"It is," the Customs man agreed. "Someone, perhaps aboard a freighter, tosses the drum into the water during the day. The amount of gas is regulated so that the drum will come to the surface after dark, when it can be picked up secretly by someone."

"Then the person in the rowboat whom we've

heard twice is a smuggler!" Nan remarked.

"It looks that way," Mr. Ward observed. "But I'll check on these watch movements and let you know."

After Mr. Ward had left, Mrs. Bobbsey said, "We're all going into River Edge to church. Run and get ready, children."

"I didn't know it was Sunday," Flossie said in surprise. "It's hard to know what day it is on an island!" The others laughed.

Later, as they came out of the little church, Aunt Alice announced that Trudy had packed a picnic lunch. "It's in the boat. I thought we'd go down the river to Stony Point," she said. "That's where a battle in the Revolutionary War took place."

The twins loved the ride. It was a bright, sunny day, and the river was full of sailboats and motor launches.

"Isn't it bee-yoo-ti-ful?" Flossie exclaimed as Toony sent the *White Gull* downstream.

After a while Bert exclaimed, "Aunt Alice! What are all those boats?" He pointed to line after line of ships lying motionless near the west bank of the river. No smoke came from their stacks, and no sailors stood on their decks.

"Those ships aren't needed any more," Aunt Alice explained. "But they're kept up here to be used in case of an emergency."

"Some of them are used to store grain," Toony added. "Occasionally one is pulled by tug down to New York Harbor, and the grain is transferred to another ship for export. People call this the mothball fleet."

"Mothballs!" Flossie cried. "That's what Mommy puts in blankets!"

Aunt Alice smilingly explained that it was just because the ships were in storage that they were called the mothball fleet.

A short time later, Toony tied up the boat at a dock, and the group walked up to the little park on Stony Point. It jutted into the river. Many other picnickers were there.

"Who won the battle at Stony Point?" Freddie asked.

"The Continental Army, of course!" Toony snorted. "Under General Anthony Wayne they captured the Point from the British in one night's fighting!"

After the delicious lunch, the children strolled around looking at the monuments and reading the inscriptions.

Suddenly Nan heard a frantic cry. She looked around. Then she realized that the cries were coming from a woman near her.

Nan ran up to her. "What's the matter?" she asked.

"My little boy! My little Bobby!" the woman exclaimed. "He's disappeared!"

"What does he look like?" Nan asked soothingly. "I'll help you look for him."

The woman excitedly told her that the boy was five years old. He had dark hair and was wearing blue jeans and a red shirt.

"Please don't worry," Nan said. "I'm sure I can find him!"

Nan walked around the park searching behind trees and in the refreshment building. There was no little boy in a red shirt.

Finally she made her way up a small hill in the woods. There she caught a glimpse of red and heard a whimper. She ran forward. Perched on an old cannon was a dark-haired boy, crying pitifully.

Nan hurried over. "Is your name Bobby?"

The child nodded tearfully. "I'm—I'm caught!" he said. "My foot!"

The little boy's foot was wedged tightly between the barrel of the cannon and a part of the carriage. Nan took him in her arms and gently worked his foot loose. Then she led the child back to the park.

"Oh, Bobby! I'm so glad to see you!" his mother exclaimed, hugging the boy. The grateful woman thanked Nan again and again.

"I'm caught!" the child said

A moment later Bert came running up to his twin. "Come with me, Nan," he said. "I want to show you something!"

He led the way over to an old lighthouse which stood on a point. It was eight-sided and built of whitewashed stones. The windows were covered with iron bars.

"Wouldn't this be a great place for the smugglers to signal from?" Bert asked.

A young park worker standing nearby heard him. "This lighthouse hasn't been used since 1800," the young man said. "There's no way to get in it any more." He pointed down the river to a tall steel tower. "That's the lighthouse we use now."

Meanwhile, Flossie and Freddie, with their mother, were walking toward the old lighthouse. Freddie had heard Bert say something about signaling, and he had an idea.

"Mother," he said, "may I borrow that little mirror you carry in your purse?"

When Mrs. Bobbsey handed it to him, Freddie ran up to a knoll which was surrounded by a chain fence. He scrambled over this into the center of the ring.

As Bert and Nan came down the path from the lighthouse, Freddie held the mirror so that it caught the rays of the sun, then beamed the reflected light into Bert's eyes. Bert looked up and covered his eyes with his hand.

"Ha, ha!" Freddie laughed. "I'm a smuggler, and I'm signaling you!"

His brother grinned. "Some signal! I can't even see it!"

"I read your signal, smuggler!" Mrs. Bobbsey called to her small son. "It said, 'I'm coming down now. It's time to start home!' "

"Oh, all right," Freddie said reluctantly.

The remains of the picnic were packed in the basket, and the journey down to the dock began. Soon the *White Gull* was headed upstream.

"I want to see the mothball boats again!" Flossie pleaded.

Aunt Alice asked Toony to turn the launch so it would run past the old ships. They were anchored in neat rows. Some of them were freighters and some gray-hulled warships. There was a ghostly atmosphere about them as they rode the calm waters of the river, silent and lifeless.

The *White Gull* was almost past the fleet when Flossie suddenly pointed to a ship in the middle of the last line.

"A man's climbing down the side of that boat!" she cried. "He looks just like Slippery Jenks!"

CHAPTER XI

FOREST GOBLIN

"SLIPPERY JENKS!" Nan exclaimed. "What would he be doing on one of those empty ships?"

"I wonder," said Toony. He asked Bert to hold the wheel, then grabbed his binoculars. He focused them on the man. "Flossie's right!" he said. "That *is* Slippery!"

"Can you see what he's doing?" Bert asked.

Toony look puzzled. "Nothing now, but that Jenks must be up to something crooked!"

At this moment Slippery Jenks was lost from sight. Again the twins wondered if it was he who had stolen Aunt Alice's antiques. "We'll have to find proof one way or another," Bert determined.

Toony steered the *White Gull* out into the channel again, and it sped upstream.

Suddenly Freddie, who was seated in the stern, cried out, "Toony! There's a motorboat heading right for us. It's going to hit us!"

Toony cast a quick look over his shoulder, then swerved the launch. As he did, the other craft sped past them. The next minute it turned directly across the *White Gull's* path. Only Toony's violent wrench of the wheel again kept the two boats from colliding!

The man in the motorboat turned and shook his fist as he raced on up the river. "Slippery Jenks!" Nan gasped.

"Goodness!" Mrs. Bobbsey exclaimed, her face white. "What a narrow escape!"

"That man should be arrested!" Aunt Alice said indignantly. "Toony, you had better report him to the river police."

"I will, Miss Conover," Toony agreed, "though I think he was just trying to frighten us."

The rest of the trip home was made without any more unpleasant incidents. Trudy reported that no news had been received from Mr. Ward about the smugglers.

After supper Bert drew Nan aside. "I have a plan," he said. "Let's try to capture another of those lighted drum boxes."

"Okay," Nan agreed. "How?"

Bert suggested that if no lights had appeared by the time the twins went to bed, he and Nan would take turns watching from their windows.

"Each of us will stand a watch," Bert directed. "Then whoever sees one of the lights will call the other, and we'll go down and try to bring it ashore."

"We'd better not tell Flossie and Freddie," Nan warned, "or they'll want to help—and they need their sleep."

"You're right," Bert agreed, laughing. "They wouldn't be able to stay awake long enough anyhow!"

No lights were noticed during the evening. When the younger twins went to bed, Nan and Bert met in the hallway and discussed their plan again.

"I'll take the first watch," Bert told his sister. "I'll wake you in two hours. Okay?"

"I'll be ready to report for duty, sir!" Nan said, laughing. "Good luck!"

Bert went quietly into his bedroom and made himself comfortable in a wing chair by the window. Several times he was alerted by lights, but they turned out to be from boats on the river.

"Come on, bobbing lights!" he said to himself. "I'm not keeping guard here for nothing!"

It seemed only the next minute that Bert felt someone shaking him. He sat up with a start. His room was flooded with sunlight, and Nan was looking down at him!

"Bert! Wake up!" she cried, "It's seven o'clock in the morning!"

"Huh? What happened?" he asked drowsily.

"You're a fine watchman!" Nan exclaimed

teasingly. "You must have fallen asleep soon after I left you, and you've slept all night!"

"Oh, no!" Bert groaned, rubbing his eyes. "That means I missed any bobbing lights."

At this moment Freddie was awakened by the voices and sat up in bed. "What's Bert doing in that old chair?" he asked sleepily.

"He's watching for bobbing lights," Nan replied with a grin and explained to Freddie how Bert had fallen fast asleep.

"Hey, this is neat!" Freddie shouted, getting out of bed. "Wait till I tell Flossie what happened to Bert!" He ran barefooted from the room.

Bert groaned again and looked embarrassed. "I'm sorry, Nan," he said sheepishly. "I was going to be such a great guard!"

By this time the younger twins had appeared in the room. They were doubled over with laughter.

"You look silly in that chair," Flossie said teasingly. "And your clothes are all wrinkled!"

Freddie's eyes opened wide. "Were you playing Rip Van Winkle, too?" he asked with a giggle.

"Not exactly," Bert answered. "But I might have slept for twenty years if Nan hadn't tapped me!" Even Bert joined in the twins' laughter this time.

There was great fun at the breakfast table as the story was told to the four grownups.

When they had finished eating, Nan said she had a request. "I wish we could go back to those old ships. I'd like to find out what Slippery Jenks was doing there."

Aunt Alice looked up. "I'm sure Toony will be glad to take you children. Your mother and I will be busy," she remarked.

"Thanks, Aunt Alice," Bert said. "That'll be great."

The children were just finishing their milk when they heard a shout from the lawn. It came from Cliff Myers. The twins looked at one another in dismay.

A few seconds later he burst into the dining room. "Hi, you kids!" he cried. "I came over to go swimming!"

"We're going down to the mothball fleet," Freddie told him.

"That's okay," Cliff observed breezily. "I'll come along, and we can swim somewhere down there."

Bert flashed Nan a glance which said, "There go our detecting plans!"

The twins, however, politely agreed to Cliff's suggestion, and put on their bathing suits for the trip down the river. Just as they were leaving the house, the telephone rang.

"It's for you, Bert," Trudy called.

Mr. Ward was calling to report that he had checked the numbers and markings on the boxes of watch movements. "No duty has ever been paid on them, so they definitely were smuggled into the country," the Customs man said. "Now we have to find out how they got into the river and who picked them up!"

"We'll keep looking for more boxes, too," Bert promised before he hung up.

The others were waiting. When Bert reported his conversation to them, Cliff demanded to know what it was all about. The twins told him about finding the drum of smuggled watch parts.

"That's not so great!" he scoffed. "I've found lots of queer things in the river."

"Huh!" Freddie thought. "Wait'll we help catch the crooks! Won't Cliff be surprised!"

As they started down to meet Toony at the dock, a thought came to Bert. "I'll meet you in the boat," he said, running back to the house. He dashed up the stairs into his bedroom.

When he returned to the dock, he was carrying snorkels, face masks, and flippers for skin diving. "I thought it would be fun to use these when we swim," Bert explained.

It was another beautiful day. As they went down the river, Toony pointed out the big estates along the east bank of the Hudson. "Several of those houses were built by the early settlers," he said. "Nowadays most of the places are used for schools and institutions."

"Ooh, look!" Flossie exclaimed. "There's a fairy castle!"

Toony smiled. "Some of the people who built houses on the river in the old days were from Germany," he said. "They wanted to make the Hudson look like the Rhine River in their country, so they designed their homes to look like castles!"

"That house must have been torn down." Nan pointed to several marble columns standing on a bluff above the river.

Toony laughed. "Those aren't real ruins," he told her. "They were built there on purpose to make the place look old!"

"People who lived along this river did funny things, didn't they?" Flossie observed.

"There are some people living back from the river who even believe in witches," Toony said.

"There aren't any witches!" Freddie spoke up scornfully.

"Well, an old lady I met up there in the country once told me a witch had tipped over her kitchen stove," Toony declared solemnly.

"How did she know? Did she see the witch?" Cliff demanded quickly.

"I asked her that," Toony replied. "She said witches always leave star-shaped tracks, and she had seen such tracks in some flour which had been spilled on the floor!"

Flossie giggled. "A witch with star feet! I'd like to see one!"

The other Bobbseys laughed, but Cliff looked very serious. He said nothing. Bert eyed him in surprise, having expected the other boy to act scornful as he often did. "Maybe Cliff really believes in the witch!" Bert thought.

"Tell us some more stories, Toony!" Flossie begged.

"Yes, please!" Freddie joined in.

"Well, now let's see," Toony said thoughtfully. "Did you know that some people used to think there was a Dutch goblin who sat on top of Dunderberg Mountain?"

"What did the goblin do?" Flossie asked, her eyes dancing impishly.

"He sat up there with a big speaking trumpet, and he gave orders to the winds!"

Freddie cupped his hands to his mouth and yelled, "Blow, North Wind!"

"That's the way he did it, Freddie," Toony said with a grin. "And if the boats passing the mountain didn't lower their sails to salute, the goblin would order the winds to upset them! There's the channel just ahead, between Dunderberg and the peak called Anthony's Nose."

"What a funny name!" said Flossie.

Here the river became narrower, and the mountains on each side loomed higher. Suddenly, when the *White Gull* had reached the narrowest part of the channel, a strong wind sprang up. The water grew rough, and the boat rocked.

"It's the Dutch goblin!" Flossie cried. "Drop the sails!"

"I'll do it!" Freddie cried. "It's a good game. Here's the sail!"

Before anyone could stop him, he grabbed a sweater, perched on the deck rail, and began to swing his signal. At that moment the waves from the wake of a passing ship hit the *White Gull*.

Freddie teetered dangerously.

CHAPTER XII

DIVING FOR TREASURE

FLOSSIE screamed. "Freddie, you'll fall in the water!"

With one leap Nan crossed the rolling deck. She grabbed Freddie's arm and pulled him back.

Freddie flopped down on the seat in disgust. "I just started the game!"

The wind died down as suddenly as it had come up. Flossie giggled. "Anyway, Freddie stopped the Dutch goblin!"

Nan laughed. "I sure hope he stays stopped!"

The *White Gull* continued on through the channel. "This is the spot," Toony pointed out, "where the American soldiers put the logs and iron chain across the river during the Revolutionary War to keep the British from sailing up."

"What's that place just ahead?" Nan asked,

pointing to a dock and several buildings on the mountainside.

"Bear Mountain Park," was Toony's reply.

At that moment Cliff announced, "I'm going in the water. Come on, everybody!"

Bert looked questioningly at Toony. "Is it okay?" he asked.

"If you can swim," Toony replied. When he was assured that all the children were swimmers, he said, "I'll tie up the boat, then you can go in."

He maneuvered the launch close to the dock and made it fast. "Dive in!" he said.

The twins and Cliff plunged into the water. They swam around a bit, played tag, then climbed back on the boat to rest.

Presently Bert tossed a mask and snorkel and a pair of flippers to Nan. "Come on, Nan!" he said. "Let's search for treasure!"

With the gear in place, Bert and Nan slid into the water. Then with a flash of the rubber fins they disappeared under the surface.

Nan was the first to come up. Bert followed soon after. He shook his head in discouragement. "It's too murky down there to see much," he remarked as he and his twin pulled themselves up onto the launch.

"Let me go down!" Freddie pleaded. "I'll bet I can find something!"

"All right," Bert said. "Use my gear. But don't stay down long!"

"I'll go with him," Nan offered.

Freddie put on the equipment, and the two dropped into the water. The other children went on talking.

"Did the chain really keep the British ships from coming up the river?" Bert asked.

Toony explained that the British had broken through the chain early in the war. "But the Americans later built a stronger one by stretching two parallel strands of chain across the river farther up," he added. "It went from West Point to Constitution Island. The British never got through that!"

"Bert," Flossie interrupted, "I don't see any snorkels. They were just there a minute ago. M-maybe something's happened to Freddie and Nan!"

The others looked startled. "I'll see!" Bert said quickly. He put on his spare mask and dived into the river. In a moment he saw Nan directly below. She was motioning Freddie to come up.

The little boy was picking up something from the bottom of the river. He beckoned to Nan excitedly. Nan swam over and grabbed Freddie by the arm. Giving vigorous kicks, the two rose. On the way they met Bert swimming toward them. Finally the twins bobbed to the surface.

"Oh, Freddie!" Flossie cried as Bert, Nan, and their little brother swam over to the launch. "I thought you were drowned!"

"I was collecting treasure!" Freddie explained proudly. He scrambled on board and held out his hand.

"Treasure!" Flossie echoed, as Freddie displayed five round black pieces of metal.

"Say, they're neat!" Bert said admiringly.

"I'll bet the British dropped these coins here during the Revolutionary War!" Freddie said excitedly, "and we'll get lots of money for them!"

"Just a minute, Freddie!" Toony said with a smile. "Let me see what you have before you decide you've made your fortune!"

Eagerly Freddie put the pieces of metal in the river man's hand. Toony examined the coins carefully, then he shook his head.

"I hate to disappoint you," he observed, "but this isn't old money. They're just ordinary five-cent pieces!"

"But they're black!" Nan protested. "They *must* be old!"

"There's something about this water that turns coins black," Toony told her. "Look, you can see the buffalo on the nickel."

"But how did they get to the bottom of the river?" Nan asked.

Toony explained that excursion boats from New York City always stopped at this dock when they brought people up the river. "The

children around here dive for coins which the passengers throw overboard. These are some they missed!"

"Diving for coins would be fun," Freddie said, quickly recovering from his disappointment about not finding a treasure.

"Let's try it!" Flossie begged.

Obligingly Toony pulled some coins from his pocket. The children lined up along the side of the boat. When Toony tossed the coins, they dived.

Bert, Nan, and Cliff soon surfaced holding coins in their hands. Freddie and Flossie had not been able to find any. "Never mind, Freddie," Nan comforted her brother, "you found the first ones."

They dived for coins for a while, then climbed into the launch to rest. "We were on our way to the mothball fleet, remember, Bert?" Nan remarked.

"That's right," Bert agreed. "How about going on, everybody?"

The others agreed, although Cliff declared the idea was silly. The warm sun soon dried the youngsters as the *White Gull* proceeded down the river. The sandwiches and chocolate milk which Trudy had provided tasted delicious.

"There are the ships!" Freddie called presently, as they came within sight of the huge reserve fleet.

Toony turned the launch toward the rows of vessels. They stood as silent as ever with no sign of life aboard.

"Which ship was Slippery on?" Nan asked. "They all look so much alike."

"You saw him, Flossie," Freddie reminded his twin. "Can you remember which one it was?"

Flossie craned her neck to get a better look at the ships. "I think it was in the last row," she decided.

Toony turned back to the row of ships farthest upriver and circled them.

"Wait!" Freddie cried. "I think I saw a man on the deck of that ship in the middle of the line!"

Quickly Toony circled back.

"It was this one!" Freddie said. Then he cupped his hands around his mouth. "Hello!" he shouted. He called out several times, but there was no response.

"If a man *is* up there, he doesn't want to be seen," Bert said finally.

"But somebody's been here!" Nan pointed to an orange floating at the side of the ship.

Everyone aboard the *White Gull* watched carefully, but saw no sign of anyone.

Finally Toony took the launch around the line of ships once more, then headed upriver toward the island. It was late afternoon by the time they reached home.

"See you around!" Cliff called. He jumped into his rowboat and made for the mainland.

When the twins ran into the room where Mrs.

Bobbsey and Miss Conover were packing, Aunt Alice was just picking up a ship model from a table. Bert caught sight of it.

"Say, that's a beauty!" he cried admiringly.

"It's one of the first models made of the *Mary Powell*," Miss Conover explained. "She was the fastest side-wheeler on the river!"

Bert watched longingly as Aunt Alice put the replica carefully into a box. "Boy, wouldn't I like to have that for my room!" he thought, but it was not offered to him.

That evening after supper the twins strolled around the grounds of the island. They sat for a while on the high bank at the south end.

"I wish we could find some more of those smugglers' drums for Mr. Ward." Nan sighed.

"And we haven't found Aunt Alice's box," Bert said. "We must talk to Slippery Jenks again and ask him outright if he knows anything about it!"

"Where do you suppose Mr. Jenks is getting all the money his neighbor told us about?" Nan said, puzzled.

The children continued to discuss the two mysteries until it grew dark. They stared out over the water hoping to spot the bobbing lights, but none appeared. Finally they started toward the house again.

"Let's go the long way around," Flossie proposed. "I like the other side of the island where that little sandy beach is!"

The moon was just beginning to rise, and in its light the trees cast queer shadows.

As they approached the beach, Nan grabbed Bert's arm. "Look!" she whispered. "There's a moving light out on the water!"

"It's another drum, I'm sure!" Bert said in a low tone. "I'm going to get it!"

He sat down on the ground and pulled off his shoes and socks. Then he waded out toward the bobbing light.

As he reached for it, he heard a snicker from around a bend in the shore line!

CHAPTER XIII

A RIVER RACE

WHO was laughing? Bert looked around in the darkness, but he could see no one. Then he peered more closely at the light on the water which he had been about to pick up.

It was a candle stuck into the top of a wooden box!

The mocking laugh came again. Bert looked up. Coming around the bend toward him was Cliff in his rowboat! The next minute he leaned from the boat and scooped up the box and candle.

"You Bobbseys are some detectives!" Cliff said scornfully. "Did I ever fool you!" He was still chortling as he rowed away.

Embarrassed, Bert waded ashore. His sisters and Freddie were indignant.

"That Cliff!" Flossie stamped her foot. "I wish we could play a good trick on him. Then maybe he wouldn't be so smart!"

"Let's figure something!" Freddie urged.

The twins tried to think of a way to trick Cliff. It was Bert who finally figured out what to do. He outlined his plan to the others the next morning. "I got the idea from something that happened in the boat yesterday," he explained at the end.

"It's wonderful!" Nan praised her twin. Freddie and Flossie agreed that the trick would be funny.

"But how can we get Cliff over here?" Nan wondered.

That problem was solved in a few minutes when Aunt Alice announced that she had invited Cliff to come to lunch. "His mother has to be away all day," she added.

The twins looked at one another. Here was their chance! After Aunt Alice and Mrs. Bobbsey had gone upstairs, the children ran into the kitchen.

"Will you help us play a trick, Trudy?" Flossie pleaded.

"What is it?" the woman asked cautiously. When she heard the plan, she laughed. "Well, I can't see any harm in that," she said. "Tell me what you want me to do."

By the time Cliff arrived an hour later, everything was ready. "Seen any more funny lights?" he asked mockingly.

"That was a good trick you played," Bert said. "You really had us fooled."

Cliff smirked. "It was easy!" he boasted.

"How about a game of baseball?" Nan asked.

"Okay," Cliff agreed. "I'll pitch!"

"Freddie and I will get the bat and ball," Bert remarked, and Nan announced, "I have to see Mother for a minute."

She winked at Flossie and followed Bert and Freddie toward the house.

Flossie and Cliff sat down on the grass in the sun. "Do you believe in ghosts, Cliff?" Flossie asked, looking very serious.

"Naw!" Cliff replied scornfully. "There aren't any ghosts around here!"

Flossie leaned nearer and whispered, "I think there are some ghosts in Aunt Alice's attic. I heard some queer thumping noises up there!"

"It's probably just squirrels!" Cliff said as the other children came out of the house.

"Come on, Flossie!" Bert called. "You and I will play against the others."

The game went smoothly for a while. Then it was Cliff's turn at bat with Flossie pitching. She threw three balls which Cliff could not reach.

"Oh, come on!" he grumbled. "Throw something I can hit!"

Flossie tossed another ball. Cliff swung with all his might. *Wham!* The ball soared into the air and landed on the dock. Then with a bounce it fell into the river!

"My ball!" Freddie cried. "It's gone!"

"Never mind," Nan said. "I'm sure there's another one inside. Let's go look."

The children trailed into the house. Bert searched a cupboard where the toys were kept, but there was no ball.

Nan turned to Flossie. "I know! I saw a ball in the attic. Will you get it?"

"In the attic?" Flossie rolled her eyes and pretended to be scared. "Ooh! I don't want to! It's so—*spooky!*"

"Aw, you're a fraidy-cat!" Cliff said rudely. "I'll get the ball!" He ran up the winding stairs.

"Great, Flossie!" Bert praised her. "You're a good actress!"

The next moment they heard a frightened yell, and Cliff came racing down the stairs. "A witch has been up there!" he cried. "There—there are star tracks on the attic floor!"

The twins burst out laughing.

"What's so funny?" Cliff demanded.

"It's only a cookie cutter witch!" Flossie ex-

"A witch has been up there!" Cliff cried

plained. "We sprinkled flour on the floor and made the star tracks with Trudy's cookie cutter!"

"We were just playing a little joke on *you*," Bert said grinning.

Cliff's face turned beet red, and he laughed shakily. "Oh, sure, I knew it all the time," he said. "I wasn't really scared! I was just going along with the gag!" But the others did not believe him.

As the children walked outside to the porch again, Nan held Bert back. "Our trick worked beautifully. But I forgot to ask you how you knew Cliff was afraid of witches."

"Yesterday while Toony was telling that story about the woman who thought the witch had tipped over her stove, Cliff didn't laugh when the rest of us did. He looked serious. I decided that maybe he believed in witches!"

Shortly afterward Trudy called the children to lunch. While they were eating, Aunt Alice began to tell them about the days when the side-wheel steamboats carried passengers up and down the Hudson River.

"That was the best way to travel during the nineteenth century," she explained. "So many boats were built and competition for riders was so great that at one time the fare from Albany to New York City was only ten cents!"

"There were lots of races on the water, too, weren't there?" Mrs. Bobbsey remarked.

"Oh, yes!" Aunt Alice replied. "I used to hear my father tell about how he stood on the dock here when he was a little boy and watched the passenger boats racing against each other!"

"That sounds like fun!" Bert spoke up. "How about a race on the river, Cliff?"

"You couldn't beat me!" Cliff insisted. "My new rowboat's the fastest on the Hudson!"

"Bert's an awful good rower!" Freddie said staunchly.

They finished their dessert of peaches and cake, then ran down to the dock where Toony was cleaning the *White Gull*. Bert told him about the proposed race.

"Would you let me use your rowboat?" Bert asked him eagerly. "And will you be the referee?"

Toony agreed to both requests. He walked over to his boat, which was tied to the opposite side of the dock, and took out his fishing tackle. "Better make it as light as possible!" he said with a smile.

"Aren't you going to name your boats?" Freddie asked. "Those river boats Aunt Alice told us about all had names!"

"That's right, boys," Toony agreed. "How

about calling your boats the *Henry Clay* and the *Armenia?* They were famous old river steamers!"

"I'll choose the *Henry Clay!*" Cliff decided quickly. "I like that better!"

"All right," Bert agreed good-naturedly. "My boat will be the *Armenia.*"

Toony was becoming more interested in the race. "I'll anchor about a hundred yards down the river," he decided. "That will be the finish line. Nan, do you and Freddie and Flossie want to come on the *White Gull* with me?"

"Oh, yes!" Flossie cried.

Bert jumped into Toony's boat and rowed away from the dock. Cliff quickly followed in his red skiff. At Toony's direction they lined up.

"When you hear the horn on the *White Gull,* start rowing!" Toony said. "That will be the go signal."

The *White Gull* moved off down the river, and the two boys waited tensely. In a few minutes the *beep-beep* of the launch's horn reached them.

"Okay!" Bert called and dipped his oars into the water. Cliff did the same.

For a short time the two rowboats kept parallel. Then slowly Cliff pulled ahead. His boat was lighter than Toony's and seemed almost to dance over the water.

"Oh dear," Flossie murmured. "Hurry, Bert!"

Her brother, who was on the side nearest land, rowed steadily and gradually narrowed the gap between his boat and Cliff's. The boys had now covered about half the distance to the finish line.

Suddenly Cliff pulled his boat to the left and headed across Bert's path. "It's not fair!" he yelled. "You have the shortest course!"

"Watch out!" Bert shouted. "We'll crash!"

Aboard the *White Gull* the other three children jumped up and down in excitement.

"Come on, Bert!" Freddie screamed. "Don't let him cut you off!"

Grimly Bert tugged at the oars. He maneuvered to the right, just enough to avoid running into Cliff.

Nan noted this approvingly, then turned her attention to Cliff. What she saw made her gasp.

"Stop!" she yelled.

CHAPTER XIV

LANDSLIDE!

NAN'S warning came too late. *Crash!* Cliff's boat crunched against a partly submerged rock. The craft hit so violently that the boy was thrown into the air. The next second he came down in the water with a great splash.

Swiftly Bert rowed over to him. "Are you hurt?" he asked Cliff anxiously.

"No, but you made me run into that rock!" Cliff spluttered. "You got too near me!"

Bert flushed. "It was your own fault," he retorted. "You cut me off."

By this time Toony had pulled up his anchor and steered the *White Gull* to the scene of the accident.

"Climb aboard, boy!" he called, reaching down a hand to help Cliff into the launch.

Bert grabbed the red skiff and held it until Toony could tie it to the larger craft. Then, while the *White Gull* towed Cliff's boat, Bert rowed back to the starting point.

On the dock once more Cliff surveyed his boat in dismay. "It's ruined!" he cried.

Toony patted the boy on the shoulder. "The paint's only scraped a bit. Don't worry. I have some red paint in my workshop that'll fix it up."

"Thanks!" Cliff muttered grudgingly. "But just because I hit the rock doesn't mean I lost the race!"

"You should have lost it," Toony said sternly. "You had no business cutting across Bert's path like that!"

"We'll call it a draw," Bert offered.

"That's a good idea," Toony approved. Then he chuckled. "You know, the original race between the *Henry Clay* and the *Armenia* came to a bad end also. The *Henry Clay* caught fire and had to be beached."

Later, as Cliff climbed into his boat, Toony called, "Bring it back tomorrow, and I'll fix up the paint." Cliff nodded.

The next morning while glancing through the local newspaper, Nan noticed an unusual advertisement. It stated that an old Dutch house on the east bank of the river was being restored. The owner would purchase good antiques from the seventeenth and eighteenth centuries to help furnish the house.

Excitedly Nan ran to find the other twins. She read the ad to them. "Maybe Slippery Jenks has sold the flute and the old doll to someone at that house," she suggested.

"I'll bet Toony would take us over there," Bert declared.

When Toony was approached on the idea he agreed at once. "I know the place," he said. "It's the old Sherman house almost opposite here. If Miss Conover says it's all right, I'll be happy to take you."

Aunt Alice gladly gave her permission, and the twins ran to the dock. Just as they reached it, Cliff came into sight.

"Oh, oh!" Bert exclaimed. "Here comes Bad News! I forgot he'd be back."

Cliff rowed up next to the *White Gull*. "Hey!" he called. "Where are you all going? Toony promised to paint my boat."

"So I did," Toony said cheerfully. "And I'll do it right now. You and Bert pull her up on the dock. You can come with us to the Sherman house while the paint's drying."

Quickly Toony touched up the scraped spots, then he and the children climbed aboard the launch. The trip across the river did not take long. Toony headed for a makeshift dock, where he tied up the *White Gull*.

Ahead of them on a slight rise of ground

stood a large, two-story house built of gray stone. A narrow path led to it through a growth of low trees. When the visitors reached the front door, it was opened by a pleasant-looking woman with white hair.

"Good morning!" she greeted them. "I'm Mrs. Forman. May I help you?"

Nan explained about seeing the advertisement and their hope of finding her aunt's missing heirlooms.

Mrs. Forman urged them to come in. "Do tell me all about the doll and the flute," she said.

"The dolly's dress has a long train," Flossie began.

"And the flute has the letters J. C. on it," Freddie added.

"They must be very valuable," their hostess remarked. "Just the kind of things we would like to buy for this house. But unfortunately no one has offered any."

Seeing how disappointed the children looked, Mrs. Forman offered to show them the house. "We'd love to see it," Nan replied.

The rooms were not yet completely furnished but did contain some unusual pieces. In one of the bedrooms Flossie spotted a wooden rocking cradle with a tiny canopy.

"Oh, how darling!" Flossie cried, rocking the cradle gently.

Just then a squeaking sound came through the open window. "What's that?" Cliff asked.

"It's a pump—part of the machinery being used in clearing old ruins," Mrs. Forman explained. She told the children that some archeologists were working here.

"You know," she went on, "archeologists are always trying to discover anything that will show the way people lived in past times. So," she added, "these men here want to find out how this property looked several hundred years ago."

The twins had been listening wide-eyed. Now Bert spoke up. "May we go out and watch the men working?" he asked.

Mrs. Forman smiled. "My husband is directing the excavation," she replied. "I'm sure he will be glad to show you around."

Outside, the children crossed a little bridge over a rushing stream. On the other side a large area of meadow extended down to the river. Here and there were big machines, some drilling into the ground and others scooping up great quantities of black earth.

"That must be Mr. Forman over there," Nan said, pointing to a tall, ruddy-faced, white-haired man who was giving directions to the operator of a drill.

The five children, followed by Toony, started

across the field. "Hey, look at this big hole they've dug out," Cliff said. There in front of them was a trench about two feet wide and ten feet long.

"Boy, it's deep!" Bert exclaimed, peering at the bottom which was covered with wet sand.

"I dare you to climb down that rope!" Cliff challenged, indicating one that was tied to a stake in the ground and hung down into the trench.

"Why not?" Bert swung onto it and let himself down hand over hand. He walked around on the soft sand, examining the walls.

Suddenly Nan screamed, "Bert! Look out!"

The next moment the side of the trench caved in! Damp sand cascaded down around Bert. The stake came loose and carried the rope with it.

"Help! Help!" Flossie ran over to the tall man. "My brother's getting buried!"

The man and his machine operator came at a run. Toony explained what had happened, then hastily introduced the children to the man, who said he was Mr. Forman.

"We'll have you out of there soon, young fellow!" he called down to Bert. Then he turned to Toony and said, "I think we can manage without anyone's going down."

The two men drove another stake into the

ground and attached a rope to it. Mr. Forman tied the shovel to the end of the rope and let it down into the excavation where Bert was standing. The boy quickly dug the sand away from his feet and legs.

"It's okay," he called up. "I'm free!"

Bert sent the shovel up first. Then when the rope was lowered again, he took hold of it himself and climbed to the top.

"I'm sorry I caused so much trouble," he said to the men, who introduced themselves.

"Forget it, son. I'm just glad there wasn't a bad accident," said Mr. Forman. Then he smiled. "Bert, perhaps, you and the other children would like to see what we've just discovered here."

"Swell!"

As the group walked across the field, Mr. Forman explained to the children that three hundred years before, the grassy area had been a harbor in the river. "Oceangoing brigs used to anchor here," he went on.

"How do you know?" Cliff asked doubtfully.

"That's a good question," the man replied. "When we first started to dig where this lawn is, we found many articles which showed us this had been a busy place. We turned up old nails, china, and pewter."

By this time the Bobbseys and their new friend had reached a field near the river where many large excavations had been made. "And here's our newest find—the original dock!" Mr. Forman announced triumphantly.

The children peered down. At the bottom of the huge hole they could see a regular arrangement of large logs.

"But why is that dock down so far in the ground?" Flossie asked in surprise.

The archeologist explained that through the years it had become covered with mud, and refuse had been dumped there. Then new docks were built on top of that until the level of the ground had been greatly raised.

"Where are the nails and things you found when you dug up the ground?" Freddie asked.

"They're being marked and will be put on exhibit in the house," Mr. Forman replied. "Would you like to help us find more things?"

"Oh, yes!" Flossie cried. "Where can we look?"

"See that big pile of damp earth over there?" He pointed. As the children looked toward it, he explained that this was dirt taken out when the dock excavation was made. "If you sift some of that earth you'll probably find some very old articles."

All the twins were eager to start the hunt. Even Cliff took a hoe and began to scratch in the dirt pile. The workman gave each child a wooden tray with a coarse wire bottom. He showed them how to shake the box and sift out the dirt through the wire.

"In that way, if there's any object in the dirt, it won't be damaged," he explained.

While Toony sauntered over to watch the digging machine in action, the children started work in earnest. There was silence as they eagerly shoveled dirt into the sifting trays, then shook them vigorously.

Suddenly Bert held up a metal shoe buckle. "Look!" he cried. "It's probably silver. I've seen pictures of old-time Dutchmen with buckles like this on their shoes!"

The other children stared enviously at Bert's find, then redoubled their own efforts. A few minutes later, Freddie found an iron hinge. Next Cliff discovered a coin blackened with age.

"Maybe, it's just a nickel!" Flossie said with a giggle. Cliff frowned and went on sifting.

"I've found something else!" Freddie cried. He held up a glass bottle.

Nan looked closer, then laughed. "That's a soda pop bottle, Freddie! One of the workmen must have dropped it."

"Well, I found the old hinge anyway," Freddie said to cover his disappointment.

Soon after that Nan gleefully came across a leather strap with six tiny bells on it. "See! Sleigh bells!" she cried.

"That's the best find yet, Nan!" Bert said, coming over to look at it.

Flossie's yellow curls bobbed as she shook her sifting tray hard. Suddenly she set it down and picked up something from the bottom.

"Oh!" she exclaimed. "See what I found!"

CHAPTER XV

CAMPING DETECTIVES

AT Flossie's excited cry the others put down their trays and ran to her side. "What did you find, Floss?" Nan asked.

Her little sister held up both hands. In one was a small clay bowl, in the other a long clay stem. At that moment Mr. Forman walked over.

"See what I dug up!" Flossie cried.

The man took the two pieces and held them together. They fitted perfectly.

"It's an old Dutch pipe," he explained. "We've found many pieces of clay pipes, but these are the largest and best preserved I've seen. This probably belonged to an important Dutch burgher at one time!"

"Wh—" Freddie started to ask a question, but Cliff held out his coin to Mr. Forman. "This isn't a nickel, is it?" he broke in eagerly. "I found it in the mud."

Mr. Forman looked closely at the blackened metal. "This is a good deal older than a nickel," he said with a laugh. "It's a florin; the coin the Dutch used in the seventeenth century."

"Hooray!" Cliff looked triumphantly at the twins. "I *really* found something valuable. Wait'll I show it to everybody!"

"I'm sorry you can't keep these things," the archeologist said apologetically, "but each object found on the grounds has to be preserved in the collection for the house."

The children looked sad, so he went on, "However, we'll put a label on each article, telling who found it!"

"Won't it be 'citing to have our names where other people can see them!" Flossie cried.

All the way back across the river the conversation was about the fun of digging up old treasures. "I'm going to be a arkologist when I grow up!" Freddie announced.

The other twins laughed. Freddie changed his idea of what he wanted to be so often that it was difficult to keep up with him.

The paint on Cliff's boat was dry when they reached the island dock, so he said good-by and rowed off. The twins ran up to the house. In the living room their mother and Aunt Alice were surrounded by piles of old-fashioned clothes.

After Nan told of the twins' adventure, she

asked, "What are you going to do with all these things?" She picked up a wide-brimmed straw hat trimmed with pink roses.

"These clothes are from many generations of my family," Aunt Alice explained. "Your mother and I are sorting them. We'll send the best to a museum so that visitors may see how people dressed many years ago."

Nan put the floppy hat on her head and bent down to select a pale blue dress with many flounces on the skirt. "Oh, Aunt Alice, may I try this on?" she asked.

"Certainly, dear."

Flossie clapped her hands. "Goody! Let's all dress up!" she suggested excitedly.

She hunted through a pile of children's outfits. Presently she held up a dress. It had a full pink skirt and a lacy white top trimmed with black velvet ribbons.

"Isn't this bee-yoo-ti-ful?" she cried.

Bert decided he did not want to dress up, but the two girls ran upstairs to change. In a few minutes they returned.

"You both look lovely!" Aunt Alice said as Nan and Flossie paraded around the room.

Mrs. Bobbsey chuckled. "I'd hardly believe you are modern-day children."

Freddie had been examining the pile of men's and boys' clothes. Now he picked up a wide-brimmed felt hat with a pointed crown. Under it was a full black coat with a plain white collar. Quickly he put on the hat and coat.

As he plunged his hands into the huge pockets, he looked startled, then pulled out a long clay pipe just like the one Flossie had found at the Sherman house. Grinning, Freddie strutted about with the unlit pipe in his mouth.

"I'm an old Dutch hamburger!" he said proudly.

"A what?" his mother asked, puzzled.

"Mr. Forman said an old Dutch hamburger had a pipe like this," Freddie explained.

Nan laughed. "He said a *burgher*—which means a Dutch citizen."

"Oh!" said Freddie, breaking into a grin.

Later that afternoon when the twins were playing on the porch, they heard a voice hail them from the dock. Then Mr. Ward, the Customs man, came striding up the path.

"Hi, there!" he called. "How are the Bobbsey detectives today?"

"We haven't been very successful," Bert admitted.

"I've just come from Albany," Mr. Ward said. "The police up there have investigated a warehouse and found it full of smuggled goods. We *must* learn how these things are getting into our country!"

Freddie strutted about with the unlit pipe
in his mouth

"Aren't there any clues?" Nan asked.

The Customs man reported that word had been received from Switzerland saying certain sailors were suspected of taking watch movements unlawfully into the United States.

"But when the sailors were detained and questioned in Albany, of course, they denied it," Mr. Ward went on. "We couldn't find the watch parts either on them or in the ship!"

"They must drop them in the river in drums like the ones we found!" Bert observed.

Mr. Ward nodded. "I'm convinced of it," he agreed. "The key to the whole plot is the person who's picking up the lighted drums at night. We must catch him!"

"We'll do it!" Freddie spoke up eagerly.

The Customs official explained that his men had been guarding the water around the island ever since Bert had found the mysterious box, but they had not seen any bobbing lights or any suspicious boatmen.

"I'm afraid the crooks know this place is being watched," he continued, "since that one box was found. So I'm withdrawing my guard detail for a while and following another clue."

"We'll take over for you!" Bert offered.

The Customs man smiled. "I was hoping you would." He took a powerful flashlight from his pocket. "Either I or one of my men will be stationed on the mainland opposite the east side of the island each night," he said. "If you see anything suspicious, just blink this three times."

After going into the house for a few words with Mrs. Bobbsey and Aunt Alice, Mr. Ward said good-by. The twins discussed what they would do to try to spot the smugglers.

"Why don't we camp out on the riverbank?" Bert proposed eagerly. "Then we could take turns watching all night!"

"Camping out is a wonderful idea," Nan agreed. "Let's ask Mother and Aunt Alice."

The twins ran into the house. After telling Mrs. Bobbsey and Aunt Alice about Mr. Ward's problem, they asked if they could camp out.

"What do you think about it, Mary?" Miss Conover asked uncertainly.

"The twins often camp out at home," Mrs. Bobbsey replied. "I'm sure they'll be perfectly all right."

Directly after supper Toony helped the children carry two old mattresses and some blankets out to the south side of the island. "From here you can see east, south, and west. I don't think those smugglers are going to work on the north side, because the current would make their drums bump into our island."

"And put out the lights," Bert added.

"Bert," said Freddie, "let's you and I put our mattress close to the bank. Then we'll be sure to see the lights."

"Okay," said Bert.

The two boys soon had their sleeping place arranged. Nan and Flossie, meanwhile, had put their mattress nearby under a spreading tree. When everything was ready, the children ran back to the house and put on their pajamas.

By the time they came outside again it was growing dusk. Bert led the way to the bank, carrying the big flashlight Mr. Ward had given him. "I'll put the light here at the edge of our mattress," he said to his sisters. "If anything suspicious happens, one of us can grab it and give the signal."

"All right," Nan agreed, and the girls went to their camping spot.

The children settled down and all was quiet for a few minutes. Then Bert stood up. "I forgot to bring that pole," he said. "We'll need it to pull in the drum if we see the light! I'll be right back."

Bert had been gone only a short time when Flossie said, "I see some lights!"

Nan looked where Flossie directed. There were two greenish lights shining through the darkness. "They don't look far enough away to be on the river," Nan said.

As she spoke there was a rustle in the bushes, and the lights disappeared. Nan giggled. "I guess it was just the eyes of a little animal," she said.

Shortly after that Bert appeared with the pole. He sat down beside Freddie. "Did you see anything while I was gone?" he asked in a whisper.

The girls told him about the lights which Flossie had seen. "There are some more," Freddie spoke up sleepily. "Right on the bank."

"That's no animal!" Bert said excitedly as he peered into the distance. *"Those* lights are moving, and they're on the water!"

"Shall we give the signal?" Nan asked, reaching for the flashlight.

"No. Wait a minute," Bert replied. "I'm going to pull in the box first!" He picked up the long pole and began to creep silently down the little path to the river.

He had just reached the shore and was about to try to snag the light, when a harsh voice hissed:

"Get out of here!"

CHAPTER XVI

AN EXCITING CAPTURE

BERT froze at the threatening voice that seemed to come from out on the water.

"Maybe he's the person who picks up the drums of smuggled watch parts!" Bert thought, his heart pounding. "I must try to capture him. But how?"

Bert's mind raced. "Who are you?" he finally called in a loud voice, hoping the twins on the bank above him would hear and give the blinking signal.

"Never mind!" the unseen man growled. "Just get going!"

"All right!" Bert yelled. "I'm leaving!"

Nan had been watching at the top of the path as Bert went toward the lighted box. The boy's yell reached her ears. She acted immediately. Grabbing the flashlight, she stepped behind a clump of bushes which shielded her from the water, yet allowed a clear view of the river.

Quickly Nan began to signal. She blinked the light three times, then three times again. She waited tensely. In a few minutes came the roar of a powerboat from the shore of the mainland.

"Oh, I hope that's someone coming to help us!" she thought.

Meanwhile, below, Bert walked slowly toward the path leading up the embankment. He, too, heard the sound of a boat's engine and spun around. The sweeping searchlight of the approaching craft streamed across the water.

"Who's coming?" Bert wondered.

Suddenly the searchlight's glare picked up a man in a rowboat close to the island. He was leaning over to pull something out of the river. Bert gasped.

The man was Slippery Jenks!

"Hey!" Bert shouted to him. *"Stop!"*

The boy had already realized that the bright light was coming from a police launch. Jenks, looking fearful, leaped from his rowboat onto the narrow beach. Giving Bert a mighty push that knocked the boy over, he dashed past him up the path!

"Stop him, Freddie!" Bert yelled from below. At that moment Slippery reached the top of the path.

Quickly Freddie stuck out his foot and

tripped the running man. Jenks sprawled full
length on the ground, stunned. At the same time
a small metal drum flew from his grasp and
landed on the grass.

"I stopped him!" Freddie shouted as he flung himself on Slippery.

"Good for you!" Bert said, running up and flopping down beside Freddie.

Nan raced off down the bank. In a few seconds she returned with Mr. Ward and two police officers. One of the policemen bent over and quickly snapped handcuffs on the now struggling prisoner.

By the time Mr. Ward had jerked Slippery Jenks to his feet, Mrs. Bobbsey and Aunt Alice had run from the house. Toony and Trudy followed. The grownups stared at the scene in amazement.

"So, Jenks, you're the smuggler!" Toony exclaimed when he saw his former employee. "I'll bet you stole that box of antiques from our dock too!"

Slippery Jenks glared at Toony. "I didn't take any box from your dock!"

"Then why were you always running away when you saw me and the Bobbsey children?" Toony pressed him.

Slippery looked surprised. "I thought you were on to the smuggling and wanted to ask me about that. These pesky kids were always around at the wrong time!"

"So you confess to taking part in the smuggling," Mr. Ward said with satisfaction. "The twins didn't suspect you of that, but I congratulate them for finally capturing you!"

"That boy snagged one of my drums the

other night," Slip admitted, "but I managed to get the other one!"

Mr. Ward went to pick up the drum which Slippery had dropped when he fell. "This is a new way of smuggling," the Customs man remarked. "Were these drums containing watch parts dropped from freighters going up the river to Albany?"

Slippery said sullenly that they were.

Freddie turned to him and said accusingly, "You weren't looking for a fishing rod the way you said, the night Bert and I grabbed you!"

The prisoner scowled. "I'd missed one of the boxes," he explained, "and thought it might have drifted ashore here. That's the first time you nosey kids got in my way!"

"What were you doing on that ship in the mothball fleet?" Bert asked him. "Were you storing smuggled goods there?"

"Naw! A buddy of mine was hiding out on that boat because the police were on his trail. I rowed downriver and took him food."

"You won't be taking anything to anybody for quite a while," one of the police officers said, grasping the prisoner by the arm.

"Mr. Slip," Flossie piped up, "why were you flashing those lights from Mount Beacon?"

"One of the freighters was on its way up the

river, and I wanted to let my pal on board know it was okay to drop the watch parts!"

Bert suddenly remembered something and thrust his hand into his pocket, pulling out a metal object. "Here's your missing silver button!" he said.

Slippery scowled. "You smart alec kids!" he muttered angrily, and snatched the button from Bert.

Mr. Ward and the police praised the twins for their good detective work, then left with their prisoner.

Mrs. Bobbsey smiled at her children. "Now that you've solved the big mystery," she said, "I think you can sleep in your regular beds for the rest of the night."

The twins picked up the mattresses and blankets and with Toony's help, carried them back to the house.

"We solved the mystery of the bobbing lights," Nan said, sighing, "but we haven't solved the one we promised to—finding Aunt Alice's box with the doll and the flute!"

"Where can they be?" Flossie said.

Freddie chuckled. "I know! The Dutch goblin that sits on Dunderberg Mountain took it!"

"Or maybe Cliff's witch?" Flossie added.

Tired from all the excitement, the twins fell

asleep the minute they crawled into their beds. Bert, however, woke up early and began to think again about the missing box of heirlooms. He hurried down to the waterfront. Toony was making some small repairs to the wooden dock.

"Toony," Bert said thoughtfully, eying the dock, "I remember there was a strong wind blowing the afternoon we arrived. Could Aunt Alice's box have been blown off into the river?"

"Yes," Toony replied, "I suppose it could have been. We get some pretty strong gusts along here."

"Well," Bert cried, "maybe that's what happened, and the box floated down the river!"

Toony mulled over this idea for several seconds. "It *was* high tide that afternoon when I went to meet you in River Edge," he reflected. "If the box did fall into the water, it would have been carried downstream when the tide went out!"

By this time he too had become excited at Bert's theory. The boy now asked, "How can we look for it, Toony?"

"The box would be pretty hard to find," Toony admitted, "but we might go down the river and inquire at the docks along the west side."

"Great!" Bert exclaimed. "I'll get the others, and we'll try it!"

Bert ran up to the house to breakfast. When he told the others about his hunch, they were very interested. "And Toony says he'll take us to search," Bert added.

"Goody!" Flossie cried, jumping up from the table.

"Go, by all means," Aunt Alice urged, "and I do hope you find the box. It would be so wonderful to have my heirlooms again!"

A short time later Toony and the children were on their way in the *White Gull*.

"Toony," Nan spoke up, "you never did tell us what the box looked like!"

"I didn't stop to examine it carefully," he admitted, "since I was hurrying to meet you folks. I just saw the box was there."

"Can you remember something about it?" Nan inquired hopefully.

Toony squinted his eyes as he tried to recall the box. "It's made of wood, and it's about two feet square," he said finally. "Let me see—oh yes—it has metal straps. There's some kind of marking on the crate, too, but I can't think what it is."

"Please, try!" Flossie pleaded.

But Toony could not remember the marking on the box. At that moment Freddie saw a dock jutting out from the shore line.

"Let's stop there and ask!" he suggested.

Toony pulled over to the small wharf. No one was around, and there was no sign of any wooden box. "We're out of luck here," he observed, and the *White Gull* resumed her trip down the river.

The next dock the searchers spotted was near a cluster of houses. Several children were playing there. They listened curiously as Bert explained what they were looking for.

"We find lots of things floating in the river," one little girl volunteered, "but all the boxes are empty!"

"I found a turtle!" a little boy spoke up. "Would you like to see it?"

Freddie and Flossie wanted to, so the boy ran up to a small house. In a minute he was back, walking very carefully and carrying a bowl in which a tiny turtle was swimming.

"I named him Henry," the child said seriously, "because I found him in Henry Hudson's river!"

"That's a nice name for a turtle," Nan assured him, smiling. Then the Bobbseys said good-by to the children and headed out with Toony into the river once more.

They rode along for some time peering ahead eagerly for the next place to stop. Finally Bert pointed out a fairly large wharf. "Let's try that one!" he suggested.

The *White Gull* drew up to the dock where a man was loading a truck with large crates. He looked up inquiringly as Toony made the boat fast and the children jumped out.

"We're looking for a wooden box which we think may have drifted down the river," Nan explained to the worker. She glanced quickly at the cargo in the truck.

"This is a new shipment," the man told her. "I'm sure none of these crates has been in the water." He shrugged and turned back to his loading.

Flossie, meanwhile, had been wandering around the wharf. At the very edge she saw a wooden box. It had metal straps around it and was much smaller than the crates the man was loading onto the truck.

"Come quick!" she called to the other twins. "Maybe this is Aunt Alice's box!"

The three children raced to her side, and stared excitedly at Flossie's find. Then the man who had been loading hurried over. He looked at the box.

"Hey, Jake!" he shouted.

An older man climbed slowly down from the truck. "Do you know anything about this box?" the first man asked.

Jake looked guilty. "Yes. It was floatin' in the

water under the dock, and I pulled it out while you were checkin' the crates."

The children examined the box eagerly. There was no address label on it, but it was the size Toony had described.

"Go on! Open it, if you think it's yours," the trucker said. "Sure doesn't belong to me!"

Bert ran back to the *White Gull* and returned with some tools. He began to pry open the lid. The others watched, breathless!

CHAPTER XVII

THE TREE TRUNK ROOM

"HURRY!" Flossie urged as Bert struggled to loosen the metal bands.

Finally the last strip fell away, and he pried up the lid of the wooden box. All the children bent forward expectantly and gazed inside.

"Oh-h!" they groaned in unison.

The crate was full of shoes!

Flossie pulled one out. It had a high heel and pointed toe. "We can dress up in these, Nan," she cried. The little girl slipped off one sandal and put on the shoe.

"Where's the other one?" Flossie asked, rummaging through the box. Then she straightened up, puzzled. "Why, all these shoes are for the same foot!"

Everyone laughed. "I guess *they* won't do anybody much good," Bert observed. "We may as well leave the box here."

"This is about as far down the river as we can

go today," Toony told the children. "We'll have to head back now."

That evening at supper Aunt Alice listened to the twins describe their adventure. "You seem to have become very fond of the Hudson," she remarked, smiling. "How would you like to take a trip on it all the way to New York City?"

"Oh, Aunt Alice! That would be wonderful!" Nan exclaimed.

Mrs. Bobbsey said she would enjoy the river trip too, so it was decided that she, Aunt Alice, and the twins would leave in the morning.

"It's too far to go in one day," Miss Conover said. "We can stay at the Bear Mountain Inn overnight and go on to the city next day."

"It'll be neat to go to Bear Mountain again," Freddie remarked.

"That's where you found the black nickels," Flossie said giggling.

When the children sought out Toony to talk about the trip, he said, "A friend of mine runs a boat in New York Harbor. Maybe he'll take you out in it!"

"That would be great!" said Freddie. "What kind of boat is it?"

Toony grinned and replied, "You'd never guess, and I'm not going to tell my secret. You'll have to wait until you see it!"

It was mid-morning before the group finally

started off in the *White Gull*. The day was warm and bright, and the water sparkled in the sunshine.

They had not been out long before Freddie announced that he was hungry. "I guess it's the river," he said seriously. "It makes me want to eat all the time."

Aunt Alice smiled. "Trudy must have known that," she said, "because she gave us a box of sandwiches and cake. We may as well have our lunch now—it's a long trip to Bear Mountain."

"We mustn't forget to hunt for the missing box," said Nan, as she took a sandwich.

Toony steered as close to shore as he dared, and the children scanned each wharf they passed. But there was no sign of a wooden crate with metal straps.

It was well into the afternoon when Toony tied up at the Bear Mountain dock. He and Bert carried the suitcases to the big, old-fashioned inn on the hillside.

As they reached the building Flossie exclaimed, "Look at the mountain bears!"

On either side of the main entrance stood a small carved black bear. "That one is you, Freddie!" the little girl said with a giggle, pointing to the one at the left.

"Then this baby is you!" Freddie retorted, patting the other statue on the head.

As the Bobbseys and their friends walked into the huge lobby, they stared in amazement. Everything seemed to be made from tree trunks! Even the radiators around the sides of the room were covered by hollowed logs.

After Aunt Alice had registered for them all, she said, "There's a pool here. Would you children like to have a swim before supper?"

The twins were eager to do this, and in a few minutes were running toward the outdoor pool. There were several other children splashing around. The Bobbseys soon made friends with them and joined in the fun.

Some time later, while Bert and Nan were playing water ball with a boy and girl their age, Freddie said to Flossie, "Let's go up and look at the hotel again. I liked all those tree things in that big room."

"All right," Flossie agreed, and the small twins left the pool. They dressed quickly, then hurried to the lobby. It was deserted. The children walked around examining the seats and benches made of polished logs. Finally they wandered into the huge dining room.

At the far end a woman in a white uniform sat at a table folding a huge pile of napkins. She did not look up when the small twins entered. Along the wall to the right were several swinging doors. Freddie pushed one open and stuck his head around the side.

"Come in! Come in!" called a booming voice.

Freddie beckoned Flossie to follow him, and the two stepped into a large kitchen. At a table near the door stood a jolly-looking man with a big mustache.

"I'm Joseph, the head chef," he announced. "Would you like a tour of our kitchen?"

"Oh, yes," Flossie cried. Then she looked up at the man. "Are you going to cook our meals while we're here?" she asked.

The chef laughed. "Well, I don't actually cook everything myself, but I'll see that you have enough to eat!"

Joseph took the small twins around and showed them where each type of food was prepared. As they passed the door leading to the dining room, the chef called their attention to some trays of frozen desserts on a table.

"Oh," cried Flossie. "What are those yummy-looking things?"

"They're frozen chocolate parfaits. Be sure to order one for dessert."

Freddie and Flossie looked longingly at the ice cream and chocolate sauce in the tall, thin classes. "I'll go see if Aunt Alice and Mommy are ready to eat," Flossie suggested.

The chef laughed, saying the dining room

would not be open for another hour. When he turned to show Freddie a collection of carving knives, Flossie went back into the dining room.

The uniformed woman at the table looked up and smiled. "Hello," said Flossie, walking over to her. "I never saw so many napkins before!"

"I have to get them ready for the dinner tables," the waitress replied. "My name is Zelda. Would you like to help?"

Flossie nodded and sat down. The waitress showed her how to fold each linen square. The little girl worked carefully and had finished a good many napkins when Nan walked into the room.

"Where's Freddie?" she asked. "Bert and I have been looking everywhere for you two. Mother wants us to get dressed for dinner."

"I'm helping Zelda fix the napkins," Flossie explained importantly. "Freddie's in the kitchen with Joseph. I'll get him."

She jumped up and ran toward the swinging door. At the same moment Freddie said good-by to the chef and started for the dining room.

With a rush Flossie pushed open the door. It hit Freddie and knocked him back against the table which held the frozen desserts. *Bang! Crash!* Four of the parfaits tumbled to the floor. Ice cream, chocolate sauce, and broken glass spread over the clean tiles!

Crash! Four of the parfaits tumbled
to the floor

"Oh! My beautiful desserts!" Joseph groaned.

"I'm awf'ly sorry!" Flossie cried, tears coming to her eyes. "Please don't be mad. I didn't mean to bump into Freddie!"

The chef became calmer. "That's all right, little girl," he said kindly. "Accidents will happen. Only I may not have enough parfaits for tonight."

By this time Freddie had recovered his balance and was busy picking up the pieces of broken glass. Zelda and Joseph ran for brooms and mops and with the children's help they soon had the floor spotless again.

As the twins left the kitchen, Joseph called after them teasingly, "No chocolate parfaits tonight! Bread pudding for you!"

Flossie, who still felt bad about the ruined desserts, smiled. "Oh, I like bread pudding!" she assured him.

At the supper table a smiling Zelda came to take dessert orders. Flossie and Freddie looked at each other. Flossie spoke first. "I spoiled four of the pretty parfaits, so I'll take bread pudding."

"Me too," Freddie declared.

Bert and Nan ordered the same, and Bert said with a grin, "I guess that squares us with the hotel."

The twins were sorry to leave Bear Mountain the next morning but Toony said they must go. He had telephoned his friend who had the harbor boat, and said the man would take them out that afternoon. The sky was overcast as they started down the Hudson, and the travelers hoped there would be no rain. Presently the *White Gull* reached a spot where the river grew wider and the current was slower.

"This part of the river is called the Tappan Zee," Toony informed the Bobbseys. "One never knows what will happen along here. The old Dutch river captains told stories of a ghost storm-ship which appeared in this stretch of water. Any vessel that didn't get out of her way was in danger of being sunk!"

"Ooh, how spooky!" Flossie cried.

A little later Aunt Alice observed anxiously, "It's getting foggy, Toony."

The shores of the river were soon blotted out by the heavy mist, and the people aboard the *White Gull* could hear the *clang clang* of a buoy as it rocked in the river current.

"I'll make for land until this fog lifts," Toony said, and turned the boat to the right.

At that moment a deep horn sounded. The children looked up to see a large gray shape bearing down on them!

"It's the storm-ship!" Freddie cried.

CHAPTER XVIII

THE HARBOR'S SURPRISE

"IT'S going to hit us!" Nan screamed.

Toony swerved and put on speed, but the huge gray ship drew nearer and nearer. Then, just as it seemed as if the *White Gull* would be crushed, the launch slipped safely beneath its tall bow.

"Wh-ew!" Bert exclaimed. "I sure thought we were going under!"

"Was it the storm-ship?" Flossie asked.

"That was just an old story, Flossie," her mother reassured the little girl. "There isn't really any such ship."

Toony explained that the vessel was probably a freighter. "Fogs come up very quickly in this stretch of the river. There *are* many accidents—we were lucky."

The fog had lifted as suddenly as it had appeared, and the rest of the way down the Hudson was clear.

The river had begun to narrow again. Along the west shore, huge rock cliffs rose straight into the air.

"Watch for the Indian Profile," Aunt Alice told the children. "It's a face in the rock just opposite Yonkers."

A few minutes later Freddie shouted, "I see the Indian!"

There in the very top of the sheer rock wall the children could make out a great stone profile with a sharp nose and chin.

"The cliff is called the Palisades," Aunt Alice told the twins. "That's French and means a series of stakes. The early settlers thought all these rocks along here looked like a great fence that formed the log walls of a fort."

The river traffic was becoming heavier by the time the *White Gull* sped under the great George Washington bridge which spanned the Hudson between New York and New Jersey.

"When will we see your friend's boat?" Bert asked Toony, scanning the many craft all about them.

"He thought he'd be near Liberty Island," Toony replied.

The twins were busy for the next few minutes looking at the tall skyscrapers of New York City. Soon the *White Gull* had passed the tip of Manhattan Island and was nearing Liberty

Island with its huge Statue of Liberty.

"There's an unusual-looking boat," Mrs. Bobbsey remarked, pointing toward a large, flat craft just beyond the island.

"That's the *River Gypsy,* my friend Captain Vreeburg's boat," Toony said with a grin.

The Bobbseys saw a broad deck on twin hulls. On the deck was a great crane. As Toony eased the *White Gull* up alongside the *River Gypsy,* a ruddy-faced man stuck his head out of a window in the deckhouse.

"Tie up to the stern, Toony," he called. "We'll tow your craft while your friends ride with us."

A sailor helped Aunt Alice, Mrs. Bobbsey, and the children aboard, then escorted them up to the main deck. There Captain Vreeburg met them.

"Welcome to the *River Gypsy!*" he said with a big smile. "We're honored to have you with us."

"What does your boat do?" Freddie asked.

"We pick up drift," was the captain's reply. He explained that there was a lot of debris floating in the harbor. "If it's not picked up, this stuff can be a serious danger to the many boats coming and going through these busy waters."

"How do you pick up the things?" Bert asked.

"We'll show you," Captain Vreeburg replied, leading the way to the wheelhouse.

"Look out there," he directed, stationing the twins at the front windows. Between the hulls and forward of the main deck there were two steel-chain nets. The captain gave an order, and the vessel began to move.

As it did, one of the nets was lowered into the water. "We'll go on until that net is full," Captain Vreeburg explained. "Then we lift it and lower the other net. When they're both full we go to a disposal point where the debris is dumped onto a barge and burned."

"This is fun!" Flossie remarked as the boat churned through the water. "What things do you pick up?"

"Most of it is driftwood and logs which have rolled off barges," the captain replied. "But once in a while we find something unusual—such as a grand piano or a garage door."

"Gracious!" Aunt Alice explained. "Who'd throw away a grand piano?"

Everyone laughed, then Nan said, "I hope *we* find something different today. We're looking for a valuable crate we lost."

Freddie was beginning to feel hungry, and grinned in delight when the captain lifted a basket from the floor and said, "I brought a little lunch for you folks."

Soon they were all munching sandwiches and drinking soda through straws. But they never took their eyes off the river.

Suddenly Captain Vreeburg announced, "The two nets are filled!"

In another half hour the *River Gypsy* drew up beside the long barge where the debris they had collected was to be burned. Excitedly the twins lined up at the rail to see what the nets had picked up.

Crash! The contents of the first net hit the barge. There were huge logs, two wire-rope reels, and a stepladder.

"We didn't find anything very unusual that time," Bert observed in disappointment.

The second net spilled its contents onto the flat surface of the barge. "Look!" Flossie shrieked. "A box with straps on it!"

"Do you suppose it could possibly be Aunt Alice's?" Nan cried out hopefully.

"Toony! Toony!" Freddie dashed to the stern of the *River Gypsy*.

Toony, on board the *White Gull,* had been enjoying a nap while being towed through the harbor. Now he sat up with a start.

"What's the matter?" he called.

"There's a box like Aunt Alice's on the barge!" the little boy screamed.

Toony jumped onto the *River Gypsy* and followed Freddie over to the rail where the others stood. He peered intently at the box which Freddie pointed out.

"I think that's it!" Toony cried. "Now I remember! The box had markings of black triangles. And there they are!"

When Captain Vreeburg heard this, he called to a sailor to hoist the crate onto the

River Gypsy. Quickly Toony brought some tools and began to pry the metal straps off the box. The children and the grownups watched breathlessly.

Finally Toony ripped off the lid. Inside the box were two packages. Aunt Alice picked one up and uncovered it.

"Oh!" she gasped in delight. There, wrapped in waterproof cellophane, lay the lost fashion doll! The second parcel contained the wooden flute!

"We found them! We found them!" Freddie and Flossie chorused, jumping around.

Everyone beamed, and the captain shook his head in wonderment. "It's a miracle!" he exclaimed. "The box evidently fell off your dock, Miss Conover, and floated down the river. But to think it was while you're here that we picked it up!"

"And now both the mysteries are solved!" Nan cried.

Aunt Alice smiled happily. "It's wonderful to have my heirlooms back," she said. "I'll always be grateful to the Bobbsey detectives." Then she added, "After such an exciting day, I think it's time to start back to the island!"

The group thanked Captain Vreeburg and boarded the *White Gull.*

An overnight stop was made at Bear Mountain, and by noon the next day the launch and its passengers were at the island.

Trudy came running to welcome them. "You're just in time!" she called. "Mr. Bobbsey telephoned he will be here this afternoon, and wants his family to meet him in River Edge."

That evening found all the Bobbseys at the supper table with Aunt Alice. Mr. Bobbsey listened in amazement to the twins' tales of what had happened during the past two weeks.

"My goodness!" he said. "I didn't realize the Hudson River was so exciting!"

"Toony says when you live in the shadow of these mountains you'll never be the same again!" Flossie said solemnly.

Mr. Bobbsey rumpled her blond curls affectionately. "I hope my little fat fairy hasn't changed too much!" he said teasingly.

Aunt Alice signaled to Trudy, who nodded and quietly left the room. Soon she was back with four beautifully wrapped packages.

"Since your father says you must start home tomorrow," Aunt Alice said with a smile, "I think this is a good time to give you the keepsakes I promised you." She handed a package to each of the twins.

Flossie opened hers first. "Ooh, Aunt Alice!" she exclaimed. "How bee-yoo-ti-ful this is!"

She had received the little blue and white tea set she had admired so much.

Freddie was next. His package contained the antique wooden flute. "Oh boy, thanks!" he said happily. His eyes sparkled as he put the instrument to his lips and blew a note.

When Nan opened her package she gasped with delight. There was the lovely fashion doll!

"Thank you, Aunt Alice!" she cried. "This will be the best doll in my collection!"

Bert had been fingering the wrappings on his present, with a knowing grin on his face. "I hope this is what I think it is!" he said.

The boy pulled off the paper and revealed the model of the *Mary Powell*. "It is!" he cried happily, turning the little ship around in his hands admiringly.

The twins jumped up from the table to hug Aunt Alice. "I shall enjoy knowing that the things I love so much are in your hands now," she said smilingly.

The whole evening was gay and full of fun. Finally the twins went to pack. The next morning they were up early making a last tour of the island. After breakfast Toony brought down the luggage and stowed it into the *White Gull* for the trip to River Edge.

After all the good-bys had been said and Freddie was just scrambling over the side of the launch, a police boat pulled up alongside. "A package from Mr. Ward to the Bobbsey twins," an officer called, handing a box to Bert.

On top of the square box was a tiny light which flashed on and off! "It's a smuggle box!" Flossie said with a giggle.

"Open it, Bert!" Nan urged.

Carefully Bert opened the box. He laughed when he saw the contents and passed the box around for all to see. It was filled with little candy watches!

Freddie grinned broadly as he helped himself. "This big river mystery had the best ending ever!"

"A real sweet one," Bert kidded.